ADAM'S RIB

ADAM'S RIB

A Witchy Brew of Christian Myth

ROBERT GILLOOLY

Library of Congress Control Number:		2011919711
ISBN:	Hardcover	978-1-4653-9111-7
	Softcover	978-1-4653-9110-0
	Ebook	978-1-4653-9112-4

This book was printed in the United States of America.

To order additional copies of this book, contact:
Xlibris Corporation
1-888-795-4274
www.Xlibris.com
Orders@Xlibris.com
106442

Robert Gillooly shows how all the essential features of the Jesus legend, including the star in the east, the virgin birth, the veneration of the baby by kings, the miracles, the execution, the resurrection and the ascension are borrowed—every last one of them—from other religions already in existence in the Mediterranean and Near East regions.

—**Richard Dawkins,** *The God Delusion*

Contents

LIST OF ILLUSTRATIONS

PREFACE

After some two thousand years, the Western world has recently seen its belief in a personal God plummet. A survey taken by the *Financial Times* in 2007 revealed that the majority of Europeans no longer believe in God or any other Supreme Being:

Belief in Any Form of God or
Any Type of Supreme Being

United States.. 73%

Italy 62%

Spain 48%

Germany 41%

Great Britain 35%

France 27%

Several years ago, *Time* magazine reported that the trend toward secularization in Europe had quickened, with the Vatican acknowledging that "parish life is essentially dead." Overall, the number of Europeans who are identified as Catholic has fallen by more than a third since 1978. And the head of the Chartres Cathedral recently summed it up: "There is a tendency to visit the cathedral like one visits a museum." *Es verdad!*

America seems to be headed in the same direction in that "almost half of American adults are now leaving the faith of their upbringing to either switch allegiances or abandon religious affiliations altogether"—this according to a 2008 survey conducted by the Pew Forum on Religious and Public Life. And "the religious demographic benefiting most from their religious churn is those who claim no religious affiliation."

And as might be expected, the scientific community in America continues to reject the idea of God. The most recent data show that, in a poll of US National Academy of Science members, the percentage of leading scientists who believe in a personal god continues to decline:

Belief in personal God (percent)	1914	1933	1988
Personal belief	27.7	15	7.0
Personal disbelief	52.7	68	72.2
Doubt or agnosticism	20.9	17	20.8

The reason for the decline in religious beliefs seems clear enough. After all, Christianity was born in an age in which all beliefs concerning God and the universe were conjecture—and superstition reigned supreme. The church viewed the heavens, for example, as a solid firmament on whose ceiling the heavenly bodies were hung as lights, certainly for functional purposes but perhaps for decor as well. St. Philastrius (fourth century) famously pronounced that the stars were brought out by God from his treasure-house each evening and hung in the sky by his giant hand—not unlike decorating a tree. His pronouncement could not take into account, of course, the recent estimate of there being some 300 sextillion stars in the universe (that's a 3 with 23 zeros), more than the number of grains of sand on earth.

There are many examples to suggest that humanity's learning curve had not peaked some two thousand years ago. Even a hundred years ago, Dr. John Lightfoot of Cambridge University concluded, with enviable specificity, that heaven and earth were created by the Trinity on the twenty-third of October 4004 BC, at nine o'clock in the morning. Today, and with thanks to Edwin Hubble, astronomers have been able to date the creation of the universe at somewhere between 12 and 14 billion years ago. And Stephen Hawking recently concluded that God was not necessarily involved in the creative process—the laws of science having accounted for that event. *y quién hizo las leyes?*

Overall, it appears that the long-standing debate between science and religion has reached the tipping point and that religion is now being overwhelmed by the findings of science. Events once attributed to God have now been otherwise explained by science. And perhaps the clincher has come with Stephen Hawking's recent pronouncement that God was not necessarily involved in the creation of the universe. There is very little wiggle room left for religionists after that finding. Then, too, in an era in which humanity has begun its journey to the stars, such improbable figures as gods, angels, demons, and other highfliers are beginning to seem rather quaint.

God's supposed role in Creation, of course, had already suffered a major setback when, in the 1800s, Charles Darwin found that humans were not the children of an ancient god, but rather the products of a four-billion-year process of development called evolution—and that humans had descended from apelike ancestors, not Adam and Eve. The biologist Richard Dawkins has noted that our evolution is about as certain a fact as anything known to science.

Today, the story of Adam and Eve is widely accepted as religious myth, but there are also inferential considerations that bear on one of Christianity's core beliefs. Because if there was no Adam, there was no fall from grace and therefore no reason to judge Christ's death a redemption. In effect, then, Christianity has lost its Savior.

So we have been disposed to believe in Christianity's founding legends for almost two thousand years but now know that humanity did not come about through a mythical Adam and Eve in association with a talking snake. Overall, the mythologist Joseph Campbell concluded that "today we know—and know right well—that there was never anything of the kind: no Garden of Eden anywhere on earth, no time when the serpent could talk, no prehistoric 'Fall,' no exclusion from the garden, no universal flood, no Noah's Ark. The entire history on which our leading occidental religions have been founded is an anthology of fictions."

The question then arises as to where Christianity came up with its founding legends, and the answer is at hand. For Christianity adopted, or borrowed, its beliefs from more ancient religions in the region—ironically, those that we now regard as pagan. The ancient Egyptian Book of the Dead, for example, was a fruitful source for ideas about trinities, miraculous conceptions, incarnations, resurrections, and ascensions. The Greek and Roman gods were the source of a dazzling array of miraculous occurrences. And it was within this environment that the Christian religion chose to compete for members, with the Christian God then becoming a miracle worker par excellence and the church a home for the popular superstitions of the time. In summary, it is fair to say that Christian beliefs did not come from on high, but rather were dipped from a vast reservoir of ancient religious myths, as were the miraculous events in the life of Christ.

A striking example of the formation of Christian myths can perhaps be found in the person of Attis, an ancient vegetation-god who preceded Christ in Rome and was later his chief competitor. Attis was said to have been born of a virgin, resurrected from the dead, and combined in his person a divine father and son. Perhaps one need look no further for the origin of Christ's persona. In fact, all the major events in the life of Christ, his heralded coming, virgin birth, divine nature, redemptive death, resurrection, and ascension were events associated with mythical personages who preceded Christ and who appeared to have served as models for his miraculous existence.

Certainly, one of the most intriguing items concerning Christianity is Sigmund Freud's research into the origin of the Christian God. After considerable study, Freud was certain that our God was originally a volcano-god worshipped by a remote desert tribe, a molten figure who, over the centuries, evolved into the God we know today—what some have called a sublime abstraction. Overall, Freud summed up the belief in a spirit world as follows: "The whole thing is so patently infantile, so foreign to reality, that to anyone with a friendly attitude to humanity it is painful to think that the great majority of mortals will never be able to rise above this view of life."

Part 1 of the book traces the origin of specific Christian beliefs, and part 2, the historic entanglements of science and religion.

Part I

The Origin of Christian Beliefs

1

INTRODUCTION

If Christians were to suspend their faith-based beliefs temporarily, they might suspect that an element of myth had crept into Christian doctrine. For surely such improbable figures as ghosts, witches, dragons, angels, imps, and devils bear the earmarks of religious myth. And perhaps the same may be said of many stories in Christian theology wherein, for example, we are told of the dead who have returned to life, virgins who have given birth, water that is turned into wine, sticks that are turned into snakes, men who can walk on water, diviners who read the future, humans who talk to gods, and humans who are also gods.

An indication that some Christian stories may be fanciful comes from the fact that they can also be found in the doctrines of more ancient religions—those that we now describe as pagan. All of which raises the interesting question of whether Christianity is essentially an original construct or, on the other hand, whether Christian doctrine is more a collection of ancient ideologies. The following pages address these questions, beginning with an overview of how the ancient gods came about.

2

The Origin of Gods

The idea of gods began when early humans sought to explain the powerful forces of nature. But with little knowledge of the natural world, our forebears could only suppose that natural phenomena were the work of invisible beings. Thus a volcano was caused by a volcano-god, the March winds driven by a wind-god, and the sun set on its daily course by a sun-god.

Ultimately, all natural causes were attributed to invisible beings, and humanity had a comprehensive explanation for natural phenomena—and a way to meet its needs. There was a sun-god to assure light, warmth, and energy; a rain-god to provide water; a fertility-god to assure reproduction; a thunder-god to protect against storms; a corn-goddess to assure an abundant harvest; and a war-god to bring victory over the enemy. And after the basics of survival were covered, other gods and spirits were added to cover everything in the human hope chest.

It followed that humans sought an association with the gods in hopes of influencing their vagarious agenda. But one could not relate to faceless, formless beings whose nature remained a mystery, and so the gods were given identities. And perhaps it was to be expected that the gods were usually modeled on their human authors, for as the ancient

Greek philosopher Xenophanes wrote, "If horses had gods, they would look like horses."

To some extent, the humanization of the gods was apparent in every culture. *The Golden Bough* notes that in Babylon, for example, the high gods were believed to have human forms and were certainly human in their fate, for "they were born into the world, and like men, they loved and fought and died." In many parts of the world, statues of the gods were washed, clothed, and fed on a daily basis as if they were human. And many cultures saw the gods as a family with a father at the head, a mother figure, and children.

So overall, gods were made in the image of humans—often from the standpoint of appearance, always from the standpoint of personality. And the gods were fashioned for local consumption. Black people worshipped gods with dark complexions, oriental people had gods with golden skins, and white people worshipped pale gods with oval eyes.

Thus the ancient gods were a representative of the culture in question. A Jewish god was Semitic in appearance (although invisible), spoke Hebrew, dressed in the fashion, lived in the area, and was strongly disposed to favor the Israelites in matters involving other tribes or cultures. The Egyptian people had the same relationship with Egyptian gods. In fact, nowhere in the world were there humanized gods who did not speak the language, follow the customs, enjoy the food, and dress in the fashion of their constituency—over and above their clear disposition to favor their own kind in any controversy. Clearly, people around the world created gods in accordance with their own needs and consistent with their own cultural settings.

Most of the ancient gods have departed the scene by now, their vaunted immortality notwithstanding. Some were casualties in a highly competitive and overcrowded field. Some fell to the sword as conquering

Healing Gods

The principal healing god of antiquity, Asclepius, with his sacred snake. Next to him is the little god of convalescence, Telesphoros.

(Hulton Getty Picture Collection, England)

armies were accompanied by their own gods. But old gods do not die easily, and some evolved to meet the emotional needs of the people, the political needs of the country, and the institutional needs of the religion.

3

The Evolution of Yahweh

One of the more remarkable transformations in ancient times was that of the god Yahweh, who first appeared thousands of years ago as one of several spirits guiding an ancient Hebrew tribe and who went on to become the ruling spirit of the Jews, Muslims, and Christians—our Almighty God.

The Hebrew god Yahweh was the end result of an evolutionary process that began with naturism. T. James Meek, in his book *Hebrew Origins*, describes it this way: "The world was full of spirits controlling and directing human affairs. Some were inherent in natural phenomena; others were the spirits of the departed. Some of the outstanding of both classes rose eventually to the rank of gods, and were given personal names; and as tribes developed, each tribe, through accident or design, hit upon some one deity to be its particular tribal god."

The prophet Moses, of course, was credited with the selection of Yahweh as a tribal god. In presenting Yahweh to members of the tribe, however, Moses did not suggest that he was the only god, rather that he was the god most deserving of worship. One of the considerations, certainly, was the presumed power of Yahweh relative to other gods. And from this perspective, Yahweh was a logical choice, for among other identities, he was thought to have been a powerful storm-god and, some believe, a powerful volcano-god. Freud, in *Moses and Monotheism*, identified Yahweh as "certainly a volcano-god" who, at the time, was thought to be "an uncanny bloodthirsty demon who walks by night and shuns the light of day."

After being chosen as a tribal god, Yahweh went on to become the god of a confederacy of tribes and eventually the national god of the Hebrews. Even then, however, Yahweh was regarded as one among many and not as a universal god. Yahweh was god of the Hebrews, just as Ra was the national god of Egypt; Marduk, the god of Babylonia; and Ashur, the god of Assyria. So initially, no claim of universality was made for Yahweh—a Hebrew god was thought to live only in the land of the Hebrews. This was to change, however, with the emergence of the Hebrew prophets.

The early Hebrew prophets were closely associated with the priesthood but functioned primarily as oracles. As such, they claimed to be in direct personal contact with the gods. As it happened, some of the early prophets spoke with Yahweh, and others spoke with the weather-god, Baal. The prophets lived communally, traveled the countryside in bands of four hundred or more, and could be consulted individually or as a group.

The actions of some early Hebrew prophets would appear strange today. Isaiah went naked and barefoot for three years, Jeremiah wore a wooden yoke of the type worn by oxen, and Zedekiah wore a pair of iron horns. In his book *Madness in Society*, George Rosen described the frenzied trances that characterized Ezekiel's prophesies:

> Of the outstanding Israelite prophet, it was Ezekiel who experienced the phenomena of early prophetism in their most striking form. He was subject to frenzies in which he clapped his hands, stamped his feet, uttered inarticulate cries, and shook a

Yo creo que estaban todos locos.

Prophet Ezekiel

The Hebrew prophet Ezekiel claimed the Spirit of the Lord often came upon him in trances.

(Etching by Ernst Fuchs, Mr. and Mrs. Ron W. Sloniker Collection of Twentieth Century Biblical and Religious Prints, Cincinnati Art Museum)

sword to and fro. Trance experiences in which the spirit or hand of the Lord came upon him are frequent in his prophecies. On one occasion, as Ezekiel sat among a group of elders, he saw a figure of gleaming light and fire that put forth a hand, picked him up by a lock of hair and brought him to Jerusalem where he saw idolatries practiced in the temple.

Prophesy was to change significantly in later years as the prophets of Yahweh prevailed over those of Baal and with the arrival of prophets such as Elijah, Elisha, and Micah. And in the process, the religious ideas of the early Hebrew prophets evolved and became more universal in outlook with greater emphasis on establishing a new social order.

Over the centuries, then, Yahweh lost his identification as a storm-god or volcano-god and became a personal god with the appearance, thoughts, and emotions of the people who worshipped him. Later still, his universality was established through the efforts of the Hebrew prophets.

Ultimately, the Christian and Islamic religions chose Yahweh as their universal god—and the evolution from a tribal god was substantially complete. Today, from his early beginnings, Yahweh has become what some have called a sublime abstraction.

Es una vergüenza cómo atraves de los siglos hemos sido engañados y cómo hemos sido tan poco inteligentes que nos hemos tragado todas estas mentiras. —

Un Taxista en Europa nos pregunta: ¿ y Todavía Uds. creen en el cuentico de la manzanita ?

4

Folklore in the Old Testament

Wow! ¡Qué retardados mentales hemos sido!

For almost two thousand years, Christians in all walks of life took the Bible to be literally true. Whatever their educational background or personal experience, people believed that the Bible was the Word of God and therefore not open to question or challenge. Did Jonah live in the body of a great fish? Was Eve created from Adam's rib? Would the world's animals fit into a homemade ark? Was there really a magic garden and a talkative snake? The answer was yes if it said so in the Bible—or if theologians so interpreted the words of the Bible.

In recent years, however, many of the cherished stories of our childhood have been recognized as myth. Perhaps the best-known story in the Bible, that of Adam and Eve, clearly came to the Old Testament by way of ancient folklore. Scholars note that the same symbolism of a magic garden and talking serpent were seen in the earliest cuneiform texts, shown on Sumerian cylindrical seals, and recounted in the folklore of earlier people long before the biblical account of Adam and Eve.

The biblical suggestion that man was modeled out of clay, as a figure might be modeled by a potter, was another conception of man's creation drawn from early Babylonian and Egyptian mythology. In Greek legend, as well, the sage Prometheus was said to have modeled the first man out of clay. *¡Que poca imaginación! Todo fué copiado.*

The Bible, then, did not offer an original concept of man's creation, but merely relied on the folklore that was extant. The legend of the great flood in the book of Genesis was found to have been taken, ark and all, from a Babylonian flood story that preceded the Hebrew account by eleven of twelve centuries. Sir James Frazer noted that similar stories on floods were rampant in the ancient world; all were thought to be the work of the gods and many shared the same elements as the Hebrew story and the early Babylonian legend from which it was taken. And the Babylonian legend itself ("Epic of Gilgamesh") appears to have been derived from a still more ancient Sumerian legend.

Se supone que no diré The concluding episode in Genesis, which relates to the general history of humankind, is the legend of the Tower of Babel. The Bible has it that God became jealous when he saw that humans were building a tower so high that it threatened to encroach on his own preserve, and so he confounded the builders by giving them different languages and proceeded to scatter them about the earth. As it happened, however, the Hebrew explanation for the origin of languages appears to have come from the Chaldeans, who predated the Hebrews. The Chaldeans apparently built a tower for astronomical observations, but through faulty construction, it toppled over—the Chaldeans chose to believe it was the work of a jealous god. The Tower myth then is another belief that came to Jews and Christians not as an original concept, but as one borrowed from an earlier religion. *Copiones!*

Other examples of Bible stories taken from earlier sources include the birth story of Moses in the bulrushes, which is that of King Sargon of Akkad (ca. 2300 BCE). The story of Joseph and Potiphar's wife is the Egyptian "Tale of Two Brothers."

Eso se llama plagiarismo.

In *Myths to Live By,* Joseph Campbell summed it up: "Today we know—and know right well—that there was never anything of the kind: no garden of Eden anywhere on this earth, no time when the serpent could talk, no prehistoric 'Fall,' no exclusion from the garden, no universal flood, no Noah's Ark. The entire history on which our leading occidental religions have been founded is an anthology of fictions. But these are fictions of a type that have had—curiously enough—a universal vogue as the founding legends of other religions, too. Their counterparts have turned up everywhere—and yet, there was never such a garden, serpent, tree or deluge."

5

THE NEW TESTAMENT NARRATIVES

The authorship and origin of New Testament narratives have also been the subject of considerable research in recent years. The latest conclusions in a 1990 article "Who Wrote the Bible?" suggest that the issue is still in doubt. The following excerpts indicate the scope of the question and the uncertainties that surround the New Testament:

Who Wrote the Bible?

It is the foundation of the Christian faith. On its words rest the very existence of the church and the hope of salvation for believers through the ages. Many consider it the only dependable and abiding revelation of God to humanity. Yet the New Testament, in many ways, is a mysterious and enigmatic collection of writings—one that has entranced, enthralled and perplexed scholars and theologians for nearly 2,000 years.

It is often called "The New Testament of Our Lord and Savior Jesus Christ." But Jesus didn't write a word of it. And while some of the writings bear the names of those who walked with Him on the dusty roads of Judea, centuries of scholarship have turned up little convincing evidence that His 12 closest disciples did much writing either. *mentiras y más mentiras*

The Four Gospels

They are regarded by many as the most sacred of Christian writings. The Gospels according to Matthew, Mark, Luke and John proclaim through dramatic narrative, recorded sayings and theological discourse the story of Jesus of Nazareth and the significance of His life, death and resurrection.

Yet today there are few biblical scholars—from liberal skeptics to conservative evangelicals—who believe that Matthew, Mark, Luke and John actually wrote the gospels. Nowhere do the writers of the texts identify themselves by name or claim unanimously to have known or traveled with Jesus. The majority of modern scholarly opinion holds that all four books were compiled from a variety of oral and written sources collected over a period of decades following Jesus' crucifixion, as the prologue to Luke suggests.

¡Qué cogida de pand..! ## The Letters of Paul

Outside of Jesus himself, no one was more instrumental in the founding of Christianity than the Apostle Paul ... And if tradition is correct, he wrote nearly half of the New Testament. His letters to young churches in Greece, Rome and Asia Minor are among the earliest and most influential of Christian writings.

For most of Christian history, Paul's authorship of the thirteen letters bearing his name was widely accepted. But modern scholarship has raised serious questions, based on content as well as writing style, suggesting that some of the letters are pseudonymous—written by others who used Paul's name to lend them authority. *hay en dia to meter em la carcel por eso.*

Another commentary on the New Testament was recently provided by a group of seventy-eight Bible scholars known as the Jesus Seminar in the book *The Five Gospels: The Search for the Authentic Words of Jesus.* Their judgment is that Jesus probably said only 18 percent of the words attributed to him in the five Gospels (Matthew, Mark, Luke, John, and recently, Thomas) and, for example, that Jesus did not teach the Lord's Prayer to his disciples, or predict that the world would end, or say "Drink from it, all of you," or control the wind and the waves, or raise Lazarus from the dead, or claim to be the messiah. The religion editor of the *St. Petersburg Times*, Thomas J. Billitteri, noted the conclusion of the scholars and their spokesman Robert W. Funk:

The scholars dispute the authenticity of many of Jesus' sayings because he wrote nothing himself, because the Gospels vary dramatically in spots, and because they were written decades after his death. The gospel writers were not only disciples of Jesus, *only* the scholars suggest, but skilled fiction writers who embellished Jesus' words with borrowed lore, passages from Greek scripture and other sources to fit the times and persuade their audiences that Jesus indeed was the long awaited messiah. "The writers of the Gospels are really evangelists, not historians or biographers," Funk says. "So, in a broad sense, we'd have to say the Gospels are really religious propaganda. What they are trying to do is make this figure [Jesus] a plausible candidate for the title of messiah or 'son of God' or 'son of man' or a figure who towers above similar charismatic miracle workers in the Hellenistic world."

At least, it seems apparent that many questions are still to be answered with respect to the origins and authorship of New Testament narratives. And there is no doubt that the Old Testament included a large measure of myth in its recountals. Certainly, neither the Old Testament nor the New Testament could be taken as authoritative in the sense intended by St. Augustine, who believed that the Holy Ghost had vouchsafed the truth, accuracy, and authority of the Bible.

St. Augustine, yo creía que tú eras más inteligente.

6

A Descent into Hell

One of the most vivid and durable images in Christian theology has been that of hell, wherein tongues of flame licked the bodies of sinners and the cries of the tormented echoed through an underground chamber of horrors—all presided over by a horned, cloven-hoofed Satan.

A number of ancient religions had envisioned both a heaven and hell before Christianity came upon the scene. Many of them viewed the universe as a house of sorts with heaven as the loft, the earth as the ground floor, and hell as the cellar. But it was Christianity that established the fiery nature of an unending hell. The Gospel of Mark refers to "the unquenchable fire" (Mark 9:42); the Gospel of Luke, "the fire of torment" (Luke 16:22-24); and Gospel of Matthew, the "everlasting fire that was prepared for the Devil and his angels" (Matt. 25:41).

Over time, the Christian concept of hell became, as Charles Panati noted in his *Sacred Origin of Profound Things*, "the severest hellhole of all, a kingdom of cruelty, an eternal furnace of physical torture and emotional torment. The followers of Christ raised the dark art of damnation to heights that prompted artists and poets to create visionary masterpieces: the paintings of Bosch, the prose of Goethe, the poetry of Blake, the *Inferno* of Dante, to name a few."

Reaffirming its centuries-old perception of hell, in 1995, the *Catechism of the Catholic Church* notes that those who die in a state of mortal sin descended "immediately into the furnace of fire" and that the church "affirms the existence of Hell and its eternity." But then in 1999, Pope John Paul II declared that hell was not a real place but rather a state of mind among those who had separated themselves from God. And so ended the Church's historical belief in a fiery netherworld presided over by a horned and cloven-hoofed Satan.

¿ que otros "Church beliefs" serán mentiras inventadas?

7

The Idea of Angels

The ancient Persian religion Zoroastrianism, founded by its prophet Zarathushtra, contributed a number of concepts to Christian and Hebrew thought. For example, Zarathushtra taught the existence of one god (where Moses had supposed many gods existed), the reality of a heaven and hell, and the presence of a Satan figure and angels.

The Satan figure grew out of Zarathushtra's belief in one god who could do no wrong, a premise that made it necessary to account for the evil in the world by attributing it to a devil. And just as the Zoroastrian god, Ahura Mazda, battled the devil Saoshyants, so did the Christian God later contend with the lord of evil called Satan—a fallen angel.

Zarathushtra's first experience with angels came about when, in a vision, he reported seeing an angel nine times the size of a man by a riverbank. Christian theology went on to represent angels as human in aspect but with the wings of a bird. The appearance of this Christian angel was derived from the Greek goddess of victory, the winged Nike—perhaps an apt choice as the primary function of Christian angels was thought to be carrying messages from heaven to earth.

The *New Catholic Encyclopedia* talks of the modern attitude toward a belief in angels:

> In the modern mind angels are considered to be tenuous creatures who, with the passage of time, are more and more being relegated to the sphere of legend, fairy tale and child's fancy. Then, of course, there was rationalism, which thought that all belief in the existence of angels should be repudiated. Inasmuch as they are considered to be products of the imagination, their existence is widely denied. The believing Christian, however, will even today maintain that there are angels because the Bible and the church teach it.

And so it was the mythology of ancient Persia that led the Christian fathers to believe in the reality of angels—improbable figures from a fantasy world, but nevertheless vouched for by the Church and revered by the Christian faithful.

Zarathushtra – a Persian prophet

Nike – the Greek goddess of Victory

8

THE ONSET OF A SOUL

The idea of a soul had its origins when primitive humans tried to explain the life force—the force that was present in a living body but absent in a dead body. They concluded that the invisible and intangible differences must be attributable to an unseen spirit, or soul, that occupied the living body. Their reasoning also led them to suppose that the bigger man must be powered by a little man inside his body and that animals were likewise powered by an internal beast of smaller stature. The little man, the little animal, was the soul.

So along with the idea of a soul, primitive humans did their best to envision it. In many cases, the human soul was thought to be an exact replica of the individual although about the size of a thumb and somewhat incorporeal, which permitted it to move about within the body. The invisible and insubstantial nature of the soul also permitted the soul to leave the body; sleep was considered a temporary absence of the soul and death, a permanent absence.

In order to encourage the soul's return when a person's health or disposition suggested their soul was wandering, some ancients scattered rice in an appeal to its appetite. Other stratagems were in place to keep the soul in the body of a corpse, lest the body go to its reward unaccompanied by its spirit. As most escapes were made through the nose and mouth, the soul was often contained by plugging the nose or binding the mouth.

The absence of the soul from the body was always risky business because the soul might be exposed to baleful influences in its travels. There were, however, safeguards that could be employed to protect the disengaged soul, even for an indefinite period. Security arrangements might include placing the soul in a box within a box, burying it beneath a tree, and assigning the tree and assorted demons the role of protecting the soul from sorcerers.

There has been no necessary limit on the number of souls a person might possess. The Caribs believed that one soul resided in the head, another in the heart, and still others wherever the blood could be felt to pulsate. Other societies somewhat arbitrarily believed that people had four souls, each of which could sustain their body, but after the fourth soul had departed, they must die. The natives of Laos count a total of thirty spirits, or souls, that reside in the body, fairly well covering all the vital and functioning body parts.

Many ancient societies believed that the soul of a person or animal was in the blood, and the heart, in particular, was viewed as the seat of life or even as having a soul of its own. The concept of a bleeding heart has been a symbol of the soul in some religions. And in part, the concept of sacrifice and the supposed bloodlust of the spirit world were traceable to the ancient superstition that blood was, in fact, the soul of the spirit.

So from early peoples up to the present, there have been infinite variations on the concept of the soul. And there are few, if any, modern conceptions of the soul that are not found in the beliefs of ancient civilizations. Christians may not undertake, as the Egyptians did, to place a little ladder or boat in the tomb so that the soul could climb or sail its way to the stars, but share other Egyptian beliefs about the soul

Ascending Soul

The soul of a dying man issues from his mouth as angels and demons
vie for it.

(From a drawing in the early 1800s, J. Collin de Planey,
Dictionnaire Infernal, Mary Evans Picture Library, London)

including a day of judgment wherein the pure soul is rewarded and the tainted soul punished in eternal fires.

So the Christian concept of a soul, as such, was born in the minds of ancient people who attempted to explain the invisible force that gives life to our bodies. And the ancients explained this mystery of nature, as they did other natural phenomena, by attributing it to an unseen spirit, or soul.

9

ASCETICISM FOR THE SOUL

Many religions have embraced the idea of self-inflicted pain and suffering. And indeed, the great heroes of some faiths were the martyrs and ascetics who, to improve and display their holiness, punished their minds and bodies. *marquintas!*

There were very early traces of asceticism in Greek culture, as far back as the seventh century BCE. But the real beginning was with the Dionysian cult, whose members went into ecstatic trances. Dionysus was the Greek god of wine and liberation and was frequently associated with fertility symbols such as satyrs, goats, and bulls. The Dionysian cult proposed the idea that the body was in opposition to the soul and suggested that the soul could reach new heights of ecstasy if freed from bodily restraints. The body therefore became the enemy of the soul, and the soul could be purified by assaulting and denying the body. Such a belief was the beginning and the very essence of asceticism.

The Greek philosophers Plato and Socrates took over the idea of the soul and gave further credence to the idea that the body restrains the soul. Other schools, such as the Cynics and Stoics, also gave thought to the idea of world renunciation and the possibilities of ascetic behavior. Roman thought on the subject reflected a general acceptance of the

Greek ideas, and from what began with the Dionysian cult in about 300 BCE, the stage was set for Christian asceticism.

Early Christianity necessarily departed from the Judaic tradition when it adopted asceticism, apparently finding its models and motives in pagan Hellenism. The ideal of Christian asceticism was martyrdom or, short of that, an imitation of Christ's suffering that would somehow result in a mystical union with God.

Christian asceticism followed many courses. Fasting had its origin among early peoples who thought that food contained evil spirits and would contaminate their body prior to worshipping their god. Sexual continence was prescribed because sex was linked with life, and the religious were taught to despise an earthly existence. Isolation was another renunciation of the world, undertaken to avoid sin and distraction and to punish the body's senses. Self-torture and pain were a way to rid the body of demons while accepting a deserved punishment for sin.

The idea and excesses of Christian asceticism became almost epidemic in the Middle Ages, as described in this passage from the *Encyclopedia of Religion and Ethics*:

> Some of the austerities of Irish saints are as follows: St. Finnchua is said to have spent seven years suspended by iron shackles under his armpits "so that he might get a place in heaven," in lieu of one which he had given away. Both he and St. Ite are said to have caused their bodies to be eaten into by chafers or stag-beetles. St. Findian is said to have worn a girdle of iron that cut to the bone. Of St. Ciaran we are told that he slept on the ground with a stone for a bolster. Of St. Mochua it is said that he lived as an inclusus in a prison of stone, and that he had only a little aperture left for letting food down to him. Of the Welsh saint Brynach we are told that he lessened his need for the luxury of clothing by dipping his body daily in the coldest water, and St. Cadoc is also said to have been

wasted with fastings. Further, of the Irish saint Kevin it is said that he remained for seven years in a standing posture without sleep, with his arm held up in the same position, and that a blackbird laid and hatched eggs in his palm.

Of course a number of religions, including Judaism, rejected the idea of asceticism and found an apparent contradiction in despising a body, or a world, created by their god. Christianity, however, chose to follow the Hellenic model first proposed by the followers of the mythical god Dionysus.

10

A POCKETFUL OF MIRACLES

The gods of old were chosen for their powers to control the elements and protect their followers—and when they did not, they were apt to be replaced by other gods. So claims of miraculous powers for a god were to be expected as well as the enthusiastic support of the claims by his priests and prophets. It was by definition, then, that a god performed miracles and thereby gained the acceptance of the faithful.

So as the godlike figures of the world were introduced, their arrival was accompanied by reports of miraculous powers, whether or not they personally lay claim to such distinction. For example, a display of heavenly lights often provided a poetic accompaniment to the approach of godlike figures and also suggested a direct link between them and the creator of the universe; thus, the sacred books of India recount that the births of Krishna and Buddha were announced by heavenly lights while stars and meteors also marked the arrival of Yu, Lao-tzu, Moses, Abraham, various Caesars, and Christ.

Actually, the birth of the great ethnic teachers was said to be surrounded by many marvelous circumstances—heavenly lights were only the beginning. James Hastings noted that, typically, "the moment of birth is hailed by a great variety of portents on earth, in the sky, or in the lowest regions. Unearthly lights are seen, mysterious music is heard. Prophecies of future greatness are made. The child himself speaks, laughs, stands, walks, or announces his intention of saving the world. Or, again, the child is miraculously saved from persecution and the danger of death. There are also wonderful signs at the death of some ethnic teachers."

Frequently, as well, the godlike figure was said to be born of a virgin and with the ability to return from the dead. Joseph Campbell noted that "modern scholarship, systematically comparing the myths and rites of mankind, has found just about everywhere legends of virgins giving birth to heroes who die and are resurrected." In addition to the miraculous circumstances of these comings (and goings), the god in question was obliged to demonstrate other spectacular powers that would at once set him apart from mortal men and women and above the gods of other religions.

And so perhaps it was to be expected that Christianity, like other religions, would bring with it numerous reports of miraculous happenings. Like Moses and Abraham before him, Christ was identified with miracles that both served to confirm his unique position and suggested a resource that could be tapped by ordinary men and women. And Christian saints followed suit, particularly in the Middle Ages, as noted by James Hastings:

> During the Middle Ages nothing seemed too incredible to be related or believed. Every saint was expected to work miracles, and miracles freely adorned the popular *Lives of the Saints*. It was said of Saint Vincent Ferrer that it was a miracle when he performed no miracle. Any saint in whom a particular district, monastery, or church was interested was apt to have many miracles attributed to him. The folk expected miracles, and miracles were freely provided for them.

Saint Brendan

St. Brendan and fellow voyagers reportedly landed on the back of an obliging whale, havng mistaken it for a small island.

(Mary Evans Picture Library, London)

For example, there was the matter of St. Xavier raising people from the dead. No mention of such a feat was made during Xavier's life (1506-1552). As a missionary in India and Japan, Xavier had never claimed miraculous powers, neither in conversations with his associates nor in the detailed written accounts of his adventures. But on his death, as often happened in the case of religious figures, he was credited with curing the sick, casting out devils, and raising the dead—on quite a number of occasions.

Overall, it would appear that the Christian belief in miracles is drawing to a close. On the desk of Father Barraqué, the secretary-general of Lourdes, a sign reads: "Do it yourself. God can't be everywhere." Kenneth Woodward, in his book *Making Saints*, comments on the current attitude of the Roman Catholic Church: "Today by contrast, the church is much more circumspect in its attitude toward the miraculous. As we will see, the modern saint-making process still requires miracles as signs of 'divine favor.' But it does not oblige Catholics to accept as a matter of 'supernatural' faith any purported miracle, including those worked at shrines like Lourdes or even those accepted in support of a saint's cause." So today, perhaps one may question what *Webster* defines as "an extraordinary event manifesting divine intervention in human affairs."

11

THE EFFICACY OF PRAYER

Several thousand years before Christ, the ancient Babylonians developed an extensive system of prayer combined at points with magical incantations. The prayer included private and public utterances, with long liturgies including choirs and responses between priest and laymen. One ritual that was later adopted by Christianity was Babylon's private confessional.

Prayer among the ancients took many turns. Some cultures began by bargaining with the gods for certain favors but holding back a portion of their offerings until the gods gave proof of performance. The Japanese, through their emperor, rewarded the gods by promoting them to a higher grade or class for particularly meritorious service. The Egyptians modeled ears that were placed in their temple so the gods might hear from a distance. Some cultures punished the gods for nonperformance, and many punished the priests or kings whose prayers did not prove effective. On the other hand, the ancient Hebrews were ordinarily very confident in their petitions and often gave thanks in advance; they also believed that people could and should ask for health, prosperity, and the good things in life. And although some of the early Hebrew worshippers knew disappointment, the prevailing attitude was that their prayers were sure to be answered.

Ancient Supplicants

A group of worshippers with their hands clasped in the attitude of
prayer, 3500 BCE.

(The Oriental Institute of the University of Chicago)

Apparently, Christianity preserved or extended the strong Jewish
belief in the efficacy of prayer. The *New Catholic Encyclopedia* refers to the
Bible as the basis for belief:

> To the prayer of petition alone Our Lord has added the
> promise of infallible efficacy. "Amen, amen, I say to you, if you ask
> the Father anything in my name, he will give it to you. Hitherto

you have not asked in my name. Ask, and you shall receive, that your joy may be full." (John 16:24, Matt. 7:7, 21-22)

There remain, however, fundamental differences among the world's religions with respect to asking for help from the gods, ranging from total disbelief that a spirit world dispenses favors to the Christian conviction that all wishes will be answered. And here at home, some discord has been noted between the likes of Huck and Miss Watson in this passage from Mark Twain's *Adventures of Huckleberry Finn*:

Miss Watson she took me in the closet and prayed, but nothing come of it. She told me to pray every day, and whatever I asked for I would get it. But it warn't so. I tried it. Once I got a fish line, but no hooks. It warn't any good to me without hooks. I tried for the hooks three or four times, but somehow I couldn't make it work. By and by, one day, I asked Miss Watson to try for me, but she said I was a fool. She never told me why, and I couldn't make it out no way.

12

THE EXORCISM OF DEMONS

In the ancient world, most religions honored the idea of demons as the cause of life's misfortunes and provided the means to remove the miscreants from the scene. Buddhist priests brought to bear fasting, chanting, and using magic castanets to exorcise spirits. Taoist priests performed exorcisms before altars to the beat of drums and smell of incense while spitting water at the four cardinal directions. In India, demons were tempted to depart a person's body with sweetmeats and sacrifices—this failing, red pepper was applied to the nostrils of the afflicted to hasten their departure. Siberian shamans blew on corpses to rid them of demons while their assistants maintained a rhythmic drumbeat and cried "Begone."

The early fathers of the Christian church adopted the ancient belief in evil spirits and provided the means of removing the offending spirits from their habitat. The priest was usually able to speak personally with the demon, elicit certain information, and then establish his authority to expel the demon by virtue of his association with a more powerful spirit.

Christian exorcism began with a decision on whether the possessing spirit was good or evil. The *Enchiridium*, a manual of exorcism compiled by a Vincentius von Berg, noted a number of tests that could be used to establish malignancy. The spirit was evil if it:

- said anything against the Catholic faith;
- fled at the sign of the cross, holy water, the name of Jesus, etc.;
- refused to discuss the possession with a priest; and
- appeared with a loathsome or dejected appearance or departed leaving a stench, noise, frightfulness, or injury.

When possession was clearly established, the priest was required to ask the devil his name, how many devils were involved, why the possession had taken place, the exact time that the devil had entered the body, and whether it was the devil's intent to stay a specific time or forever.

Then there was the Christian *Thesaurus Exorcismorum,* which described the proper approach to any possession by evil spirits. Included were exorcisms to protect a house from demons, to stabilize a marriage where the devil was at work, to cure sicknesses of all descriptions, to ward off insects such as locusts, and to avoid a cow going dry. There were also the more exotic complaints of some who required spiritual remedies against succubus and incubus demons. And of course, the ritual of baptism exorcised demons from the newborn.

The early Christian ceremonies to exorcise demons were relatively simple and involved a litany, prayers, and the laying on of hands. Origen, in the third century CE, credited the letters of the word *Jesus* with expelling evil spirits from countless people whose souls were possessed simply by virtue of the power of the name. But in some cases, strong language was used to revile the demon as a "lean sow, mangy beast, dingy collier, swollen toad, or lousy swineherd." Fumigation was used on occasion, as was flagellation; some religious authorities in the 1600s recommended moderate flagellation of the afflicted not so much to expel the demons as to show contempt for them.

Anthony's Demons

Schongauer's *Temptation of St. Anthony* illustrates the struggles of the saint against the demons who reportedly sought to overcome him.

(The British Museum, London)

Exorcism has been practiced by Christians since the church was founded and was undiminished over many centuries based on the New Testament accounts: "In my name shall they cast out devils" (Mark 16:17; also Luke 9:1, 10:17). Today, however, most Protestant denominations have rejected the idea of demonic possession and exorcism. And in 1993, the chair of theology at Notre Dame University called the Church's historical views on demonic possession "an embarrassment."

Nevertheless, the Roman Catholic Church maintains its belief in the concepts. In 1947, Francis Cardinal Spellman wrote the introduction to the *Rituale Romanum*, which was a verbatim reproduction of the rite of exorcism printed in 1619. The entire rite is shown in the *Encyclopedia of Witchcraft and Demonology*. A long and impressive ceremony, it begins by imploring God's grace against the "wicked dragon" and a demand to the possessing spirit to "tell me thy name, the day, and the hour of thy going out, by some sign."

13

THE WONDERS OF WATER

B aptism is a religious rite that traces back to the earliest of times. Early humans saw the cleansing power of water and supposed that evil spirits could be washed from the body in the same manner as dirt. In time, the presumed powers of water became accepted and expanded to include washing away the enervating effects of sin and moral guilt. The use of water in baptismal rites has ranged from sprinkling to total submersion; its source from small vessels of holy water in temples to the sacred Ganges and the mighty oceans of the world.

Spittle has also been commonly used in baptismal rites. With the intention of establishing kinship with the newborn, indigenes spat upon the infant and rubbed their saliva into the body. Muhammad reportedly used spittle in baptizing one of his children, and folk custom in medieval Europe held that spittle was particularly efficacious in keeping witches and fairies at bay and in counteracting the evil eye. Traditionally, the Roman Catholic Church provided for the use of spittle in baptismal rites, but discontinued the practice in the 1960s. The baptism of infants reflected the superstition that infants were particularly vulnerable to demons, a belief that may have been occasioned by the high infant mortality rates in ancient times. Some people were reluctant even to acknowledge a newborn infant for seven days because so many died at birth; the departed infants were thought to have been ghost babies whom the spirits had reclaimed. Similarly, some European peasants were concerned that fairies would steal healthy babies and replace them with changelings, who had puny little bodies. So the belief in devils, witches, and fairies led to a defense by baptism.

Today, there is no agreement on infant baptism within the Christian community. Some denominations baptize newborns; others believe that children should not be baptized until they are old enough to decide things for themselves. Quakers do not practice water baptism at all, and Catholics believe that infants who die without baptism cannot enter heaven, but are destined to stay forever in limbo. The Catholic doctrine of original sin holds that all newborn infants inherit the sins of Adam and, without the redemption of baptism, are doomed never to see God.

¡Qué barbaridad! Cretinos!

The origin of Christian baptismal rites, then, may be traced to the ancient superstition that evil spirits exist and can be washed—exorcised—from the bodies of the newborn with water. To this, some religions added the complementary idea that baptism could cleanse the child from impurities, taboos, or inherited sin.

14

THE CONCEPT OF ORIGINAL SIN

The theory of primal sin began not with Christianity but with the Orphic movement in ancient Greece near the fifth century BCE. Orpheus was a mythical Greek hero endowed with superhuman musical abilities whose adventures included charming Hades, king of the underworld. From Orpheus, and subsequently in the philosophic schools of ancient Greece, was born a mystic Greek religion that offered to purify the soul from innate, or inherited, evil. The Greek playwright Euripides (485-406 BCE) summed it up: "The gods visit the sins of the fathers upon the children."

The actual sin of Adam is generally believed by Christians to involve sex, and Adam's disobedience in eating fruit from the "tree of forbidden knowledge" is a metaphor for knowing Eve in the biblical sense. St. Augustine, in his *City of God*, included a chapter titled "Were Adam and Eve Troubled by Passion before They Ate of the Tree of Knowledge?"

The idea of original sin was not explicitly mentioned in the Old Testament, and in the New Testament, it was St. Paul who first alluded to the transmission of hereditary guilt from the first man (Adam) to the entire human race: "Through the disobedience of one man the rest were constituted sinners" (Rom. 5:19). As a concept, original sin found acceptance among the church fathers because the sacrificial death of Christ was thereby exalted, and the blame for human misfortune transferred from a beneficent God to an errant Adam.

The concept of original sin, then, began with the mythical Greek hero, Orpheus, and flowered in an ancient Greek religion before being adopted by Christianity via the New Testament writings of St. Paul. The Christian version of the myth used the misadventure of Adam and Eve as the explanation for humanity's Fall.

15

A Legendary Fall

The suggestion that the Christian Fall was mythical first came from scholars who studied the origins of ancient myths. They found stories of a prototypical Fall long before the Old Testament and the biblical account of Adam and Eve. Joseph Campbell, in his book *Myths to Live By*, finds "the symbolism of the serpent, tree and garden of immortality already in the earliest cuneiform texts, depicted on old Sumerian cylinder seals and represented even in the arts and rites of primitive village folk throughout the world."

In the past century, more evidence surfaced to show that the Christian Fall was mythical in nature. Scholars found in the Ninevite records confirmation that the Christian Fall legend was first adopted from more ancient sources by the Jews and by them transmitted to Christianity.

An indication of the mythical nature of the Fall stories may perhaps be seen from the description of what life was like before the Fall, quite marvelously like the following:

- A Christian version of the Fall legend spoke of human beings who were created perfect in every respect—when they first appeared on earth. There was no sin or pain or disappointment because the Creator had fashioned humans to perfection. There was even no death, for humans (and animals) were created to live forever by the grace and power of a supreme being. *y donde ponían a todo esa gente y animales que seguían viviendo eternamente?*

- The prophet Zarathushtra (sixth century BCE) preached a Fall in the ancient Persian religion, wherein the god Ahura Mazda created a perfect world entirely free of pain and despair, but his perfect creation was then marred by an opposing evil spirit, Angra Minyu, who brought about a Fall and introduced evil and ignorance into the world. Zoroastrianism was still able to offer, like Christianity, hope for a better tomorrow through the intercession of a savior, Saoshyant, who promised the resurrection of the body after death and thereafter a purified soul, both of which would enjoy an eternal life.

- Greek mythology also had its legend of a Fall wherein Hesiod (eighth century BCE) reported a revelation that men in the most ancient times were "a golden race" who lived like gods, without cares, labor, or illnesses, and were surrounded by fruitful fields and flocks; and when they died, it was as if they were only overcome by sleep. But then came the well-known Pandora who opened a vase bidden by divine command to remain closed and let loose a torrent of troubles, sorrows, and disease in the world. The problems in the world, then, have long been associated with a failure not of the gods but of humans such as Pandora and, of course, Adam.

One may marvel that people in all walks of life would believe in a literal Garden of Eden, a serpent that could talk, and a fruit with marvelous properties for the better part of two thousand years. But such is the nature of myth.

Today, Christians must contend with the awkward, but widespread, belief that the story of a Fall, credited for centuries, was dipped from a vast reservoir of religious myth. If that is the case, there was no Adam, no fall from grace, and therefore no reason for Christ's death to be judged a redemption. So a great deal of Christian doctrine depends on a mythical Garden of Eden.

16

The Rite of Communion

Ancient worshippers often consumed their gods sacramentally, eating either the animal or human who represented the god or sometimes an image of the god made from bread. The origin of this religious custom is explained in *The Golden Bough*:

> The reasons for this partaking of the body of the god are, from the primitive standpoint, simple enough. The savage commonly believes that by eating the flesh of an animal or man he acquires not only the physical, but even the moral and intellectual qualities which were characteristic of that animal or man; so when the creature is deemed divine, our simple savage naturally expects to absorb a portion of its divinity, along with its material substance.

The concept that a person could absorb animal characteristics is reflected in an early belief in sympathetic magic. *The Golden Bough* cites examples such as Caribs who abstained from eating pigs lest they should have the small eyes of a pig. In northern India, natives believed that eating the eyes of owls would help them to see in the dark. Some natives of northern Australia thought that eating the flesh of a kangaroo

Early Communion

Many early peoples believed they would magically absorb the
characteristics of the animals or humans or gods that they consumed.

(Mary Evans Pictures, London)

would make them jump higher and run faster. The Turks of Central Asia fed their children the tongues of birds to help them learn to speak.

There were many examples where human sacrifices were accompanied by participants eating the victim in a ceremonial fashion. From this, Westermarck saw an obvious parallel between communion and the sacrificial form of cannibalism:

> The sacrificial form of cannibalism obviously springs from the idea that a victim offered to a supernatural being participates in his sanctity and from the wish of the worshiper to transfer to himself something of its benign virtue. So also the divine qualities of a man-god are supposed to be assimilated by the person who eats his flesh or drinks his blood. This was the idea of the early Christians concerning the Eucharist.

Early Christians no doubt inherited their beliefs about communion from the ancient Romans whose corn-god and wine-god were represented by bread and wine that, when consumed, let the worshipper share in the divine attributes of the gods. Notwithstanding, Cicero found reason to comment on the belief: "When we call corn Ceres and wine Bacchus, we use a common figure of speech; but do you imagine that anybody is so insane as to believe that the things he feeds upon is a god?"

Although earlier Christians regarded the Eucharist as the actual body and blood of a man-god, Christ, the Protestants began to raise questions in the sixteenth century when Martin Luther challenged the papacy on the reality of transubstantiation (that during mass the bread and wine literally became the body and blood of Jesus). Currently, most of the Catholic laity in America, if not the clergy, believe that the sacrament of Holy Communion is a symbolic reminder of Christ, not his actual body and blood. In fact, a *New York Times*/CBS poll taken in April 1994 noted that only one of three American Catholics believe in transubstantiation, so a core belief of Christianity has changed markedly over the centuries.

Communion, then, represents another Christian belief that began among early peoples and gained stature over time. But its origin was in sympathetic magic and the curious assumption that a person absorbed the characteristics of the animals, humans, or gods that he or she consumed.

17

THE CELEBRATION OF CHRISTMAS

It was not mere coincidence that in the Roman Empire, the twenty-fifth of December was celebrated both as the birth date of Mithra (the Unconquered Sun) and his competitor Christ (the Sun of Righteousness). Mithra was an Indo-Iranian sun-god said to have been born of the great Oriental goddess the Semites called the Heavenly Virgin, and as a sun-god, his birthday was reckoned by the Julian calendar to be on the winter solstice, or December 25. Because the Gospels say nothing as to the day of Christ's birth, the early Church did not celebrate the event. But by the beginning of the fourth century, *The Golden Bough* notes that "it appears that the Christian church chose to celebrate the birthday of its Founder on the twenty-fifth of December in order to transfer the devotion of the heathen Sun to him who was called the Sun of Righteousness."

The Golden Bough notes as well that Christianity's Easter is celebrated on the date of the resurrection of Attis, a Roman vegetation-god who was said to have been born of a virgin and who combined in himself a divine father and son. Attis, like Mithra, preceded Christ but remained a strong contender with Christ in the early days of the Roman Empire.

In addition to Christmas and Easter, the festivals of St. George and St. John replaced ancient pagan festivals, the festival of the assumption of the Virgin Mary replaced the festival of Diana, and the feast of All Souls was a continuation of an old heathen feast of the dead. Many Christian holy days, then, were overlays on the birth date of their mythical predecessors.

18

The Star of Bethlehem

The story of Jesus often begins as the Magi wend their way through the desert night, guided by the Star of the Nativity. And certainly, a bright star was an apt symbol to announce the coming of Christ, the Light of the World.

The origin of the idea, however, goes farther back in time. Ancient religions often chose to associate the coming of their godlike figures with stars and meteors, which provided a poetic accompaniment to their appearance and suggested that heaven itself had heralded their coming.

Andrew Dickson White noted the old world belief that stars and meteors presaged happy events, "especially the births of gods, heroes and great men." And it became something of an unspoken tradition for such figures to first appear on earth amidst or announced by heavenly lights. The sacred books of India recount that the births of Krishna and Buddha were announced by heavenly lights. In China, sacred books noted the appearance of heavenly lights before the birth of Yu, the founder of the first dynasty, and also of the wise man, Lao-tzu. Jewish legend has a star appearing before the birth of Moses, and when Abraham was born, the occasion was marked by a new star in the east. The tradition of heavenly lights was found in Greek and Roman legends as well, such as in the birth of various Caesars. And of course, the sacred books of Christianity report that a star, rising in the east, heralded the coming of Christ.

As heavenly lights presage happy events, so did eclipses foretell tragedy. The Greeks believed that darkness befell the earth on the death of Prometheus, Hercules, and Alexander the Great. The Romans believed the world was dark for six hours at the death of Romulus, and the lights went out again when Julius Caesar died. One of the Christian legends surrounding the Crucifixion reported six to nine hours of darkness over the globe, and Jewish tradition noted a three-day period of darkness when the books of the law were translated into Greek—a profanity.

So in the ancient world, the coming of great men and godlike figures was often presaged by heavenly lights, and their going accompanied by a global darkness. The star that heralded the coming of Christ appears to have followed in these ancient footsteps.

19

The Virgin Birth of Christ

O ne of the most common ideas in ancient folklore is found in the supernatural birth of great men and gods. Their coming was often heralded by heavenly lights and their arrival marked by a virgin birth, further evidence of their extraordinary nature.

A virgin birth was said to occur when a mortal woman was somehow impregnated by a divine father in a supernatural, rather than a natural, manner. Thus Alexander the Great, whose father was said to be the god Zeus, was the product of a virgin birth. Similarly, the Greek philosopher Plato, the Greek mathematician Pythagorus, and the Roman emperor Augustus were thought by many to be sons of the god Apollo and, therefore, products of a virgin birth. And even though these same births could be proved natural, with human fathers in evidence, many people chose to believe that such greatness in a man must be the result of a celestial father.

Religious figures were also often associated with the miracle of a virgin birth, supporting their claim to divinity or something close to it. In his second coming, Buddha was said to have been born miraculously, and virgin births were also ascribed to the god Horus in Egypt, Krishna in India, and Zoroaster, the prophet and founder of Zoroastrianism.

Other virgin births predating Christ included that of Attis, a Roman vegetation-god, and Mithra, an Indo-Iranian sun-god. Attis was said to be born of the virgin Nana, and Mithra's divine sun was born of a goddess the Semites called the Heavenly Virgin. Both Attis and Mithra overlapped the coming of Christ.

So in pre-Christian times, many lands lay claim to the virgin birth of their culture heroes. However, they were then obliged to explain the process by which their hero had arrived, and a number of memorable accounts came forth. In the case of Buddha, he was said to have entered his mother's womb in the shape of a white elephant. Fo-hi, who founded the Chinese Empire, was said to have been conceived by a virgin who ate a flower clinging to her bathing garment. Attis, the Roman vegetation-god, was conceived when his virgin mother put a ripe almond in her bosom. And the mortal virgin Danaë was impregnated by Zeus, who presented himself to her in the form of a shower of gold.

In classical antiquity, then, there was a history of great men and gods arriving by way of a virgin birth. And the virgin birth of Christ appeared to follow an ancient tradition in that it was a god, the Holy Ghost, that breathed the figurative seed of Christ into the Virgin Mary's womb.

20

THE DIVINITY OF CHRIST

Although it may be natural for Christians to think of Christ's divinity as a unique occurrence, he was not alone in this distinction. Individuals who combined the human and divine in themselves have graced the pages of religious history from early times, and Christ was but one in the procession.

The idea of a man-god began when certain charismatic individuals demonstrated exceptional abilities, or lay claim to them, and were thereby able to gain ascendancy over their fellow men. It was the same enabling circumstance that brought forth high priests, magicians, and medicine men in early societies.

The concept of living gods flourished in an ancient world that posted no boundaries on religious beliefs. In Babylonia, a long succession of rulers were deified in their lifetime following the death of Sargon in 2800 BCE. The ancient kings of Egypt claimed divine authority over all lands and nations. The Aztec king Montezuma was worshipped as a man-god during his reign. Brahmin priests were considered to be human gods with the power to control the immortal gods and, if necessary, to create new ones. Buddha, who was not viewed as a god during his lifetime, was proclaimed a human god by the Mahayanists following his death.

In the year 646, the emperor of Japan was recognized as a man-god and ruler of the universe, and the Dalai Lama of Lhasa, Tibet, has long been regarded as a living god whose divine and immortal spirit at death is born again in a child.

Living gods, then, were common in the ancient world and so paved the way for the coming of Christ. In 307 BCE, Athenians gave divine honors to Demetris Poliorcetes and his father while alive under the title of the Savior Gods. The Roman senate enrolled Julius Caesar among the gods after his assassination in 44 BCE, and some parts of the Roman Empire deified Augustus, Caesar's successor, while he was still alive. In the first century, the emperors Caligula and Domitian claimed godhood while alive, following which all the early Roman emperors were considered for a place among the gods.

Thus human gods were familiar figures in the Roman Empire—before and after the coming of Christ—with many well-known names in evidence. During his life, nevertheless, Christ was recognized as a man-god only by his followers and not by the Jewish religious establishment or by the Roman government. It was in the fourth century, under the emperor Constantine, when Christianity became the state religion of the Roman Empire that Jesus was proclaimed a man-god by the Roman senate.

21

THE SACRIFICE OF CHRIST

Scholars believe that human sacrifice may have begun when early humans saw death all around them, supposed that powerful spirits were calling for these deaths, and decided to satisfy the appetite of the gods with somebody else—a survival strategy. Such is the explanation offered by the noted anthropologist, Westermarck: "When men offer the lives of their fellowmen in sacrifice to their gods, they do so, as a rule, in the hope of thereby saving their own." He describes it as a form of life insurance and not so much an act of wanton cruelty as an absurdity.

In time, human sacrifice came to be thought of as a gift to the gods and, as such, was used to atone for sins and allay guilt to secure advantages for one's self or community and even to serve as a ransom paid to the devil—for the ancients were obliged to deal with the evil spirits as well as the benign.

The belief in the efficacy of human sacrifice became widespread in the ancient world, and there is no doubt that such beliefs were carried forward to the time of Christ. Early Christians, then, were led to suggest that the demise of Christ was a sacrificial death offered as atonement for human sin. And it was this scenario that served to transform his death from an unremarkable execution into a holy sacrifice that would save humankind.

Some note may be given to the ancient custom of Semitic kings to sacrifice their sons for cause. *The Golden Bough* quotes Philo of Byblos, whose work on the Jews speaks of the custom:

> It was an ancient custom in a crisis of great danger that the ruler of a city or nation should give his beloved son to die for the whole people, as a ransom offered to the avenging demons; and the children thus offered were slain with mystic rites. So Cronus, whom the Phoenicians call Israel, being king of the land and having an only-begotten son called Jeoud [for in the Phoenician tongue Jeoud signifies "only begotten"], dressed him in royal robes and sacrificed him upon an altar in a time of war, when the country was in great danger from the enemy.

This ancient custom of Semitic kings is of interest because it bears a resemblance to the death of Christ, also a beloved son, who was sacrificed for the whole people—and some thought as a defense against the devil. In fact, Westermarck noted that the Greek church and the most important Western fathers believed that the sacrifice of Christ was a ransom paid to the devil, that his onslaughts against humanity might be eased. In the end, the church fathers chose to regard Christ's death as atonement for human sin, not as a ransom paid to the devil, but the choice was not an easy one and both options bore the signs of ancient superstition.

22

ON THE TRANSFER OF SIN

One of the foundational beliefs in Christianity is that the death of Christ delivered the peoples of the world from sin. It found expression in the Catholic prayer, "Lamb of God, who hath taken away the sins of the world, have mercy on us." However, the presumed ability to transfer sins did not begin with Christianity and indeed had been in the human hope chest for many centuries before Christ. *The Golden Bough* notes that the transfer of sin to a dying god had become a custom among the ancients, and there seems little doubt that the church fathers adopted the ancient belief and associated it with the death of Christ: "The accumulated misfortunes and sins of the whole people are sometimes laid upon the dying god, who is supposed to bear them away forever, leaving the people innocent and happy." Such a notion concerning the transference of sin "arises from a very obvious confusion between the physical and the mental, between the material and the immaterial." Early humans evidently believed it possible to shift their sin and suffering to another, just as a load of wood or stone might be shifted to another carrier.

The assumed transfer of sin was not confined to gods but extended to animals, humans, and even inanimate objects. A tribe in Borneo, for example, annually sent a little boat, a bark, to sea laden with the sins and sorrows of its citizenry, who then retired to their island homes to await another year's accumulation.

Animals were often used as scapegoats as in Arabia where a camel was walked through a town struck with pestilence so that it could absorb the disease; the camel was then strangled with the assumption that the pestilence died with the beast. In certain African tribes, monkeys or rats were paraded through the village to attract evil spirits and then crucified to save the entire community from demonic attacks. Jewish high priests laid hands on the head of a goat to transfer the sins of the children of Israel to the goat, which was then banished into the wilderness. And one Pacific tribe used turtles as their object of absolution.

And on occasion, the animals used as scapegoats were deemed divine. In India, Brahmans transferred the sins of the people into a sacred cow, after which the cow—and therefore the sins—were dispatched to an appointed place. Ancient Egyptians avoided sin and misfortune in a similar fashion, laying such evils on the heads of sacred bulls.

Humans sometimes chose gods as their scapegoats, but the honor was also bestowed on man-gods. Among the many was a man-god the ancient Aztecs believed absolved them of their sins—well before the Spaniards arrived with their own incarnation. And in the Eastern Caucasus, man-gods thought to be possessed of a divine spirit were slain by a sacred spear thrust into their sides while in the purification ceremony that followed, the attendees had their sins taken away.

The suggestion that Christ's sacrifice had taken away the sins of the world, then, was not a novel idea at the time. It seems that humanity has always sought to rid itself of sin, guilt, and sorrow and found the means in the magical transference of evil. Sin has been transferred to goats, men, and gods and has been sent to sea in little boats.

And so when early Christians were presented with a dying man-god, they followed an ancient custom and assigned their sins to Christ—and as Christ died, so did their sins die with him. Or so they believed.

23

THE RESURRECTION OF CHRIST

The concept of a resurrection had its remarkable beginning when early people noted that in the change of seasons, the earth's vegetation died and, later in the year, came back to life—a resurrection. It followed that the resurrection concept was closely associated with vegetation-gods, but later included other divinities as well.

Joseph Campbell once noted that the ancient world was chock-full of tales of resurrections: "Modern scholarship, systematically comparing the myths and rites of mankind, has found just about everywhere legends of virgins giving birth to heroes who die and are resurrected." The Aztecs of Mexico—and in the pre-Christian past, the Buddhists and Jains—the resurrection of Osiris in Egypt, Tammuz in Mesopotamia, Adonis in Syria, and Dionysus in Greece were among others who gave to the early Christians models for the resurrection of Christ.

Of particular significance to Christians was the resurrection of the Roman vegetation-god Attis, who was dated to about 200 BCE and overlapped the coming of Christ. When Attis died each year, a period of mourning took place, but this was followed by a joyous celebration. Sir James Frazer describes the pagan event in *The Golden Bough*:

Christ's Resurrection

Detail of Piero della Francesca's painting of Christ rising triumphant from the tomb, thereby offering all Christians the hope of eternal life.

(Courtesy of Museo Civico, Sansepolero, Italy)

The sorrow of the worshipers was turned to joy. For suddenly a light shone in the darkness: the tomb was opened: the god has risen from the dead; and as the priest touched the lips of the weeping mourners with balm, he softly whispered in their ears the glad tidings of salvation. The resurrection of the god was hailed by his disciples as a promise that they too would issue triumphant from the corruption of the grave. On the morrow, the twenty-fifth day of March, which was reckoned the vernal equinox, the divine resurrection was celebrated with a wild outburst of glee.

Frazer observed that "Christians and pagans alike were struck by the remarkable coincidence between the death and resurrection of their respective deities." It may not have gone unnoticed as well that both Christ and his predecessor Attis were said to have been born of a virgin and in themselves were said to combine a divine father and son.

The bodily resurrection of Jesus remains one of the foundational beliefs of Christianity. For if Jesus was not resurrected according to scriptural accounts, then the Bible is in error and the divinity of Christ disputable—and our own hopes for a resurrection greatly diminished. And yet this is the conclusion reached by a group of eminent Bible scholars called the Jesus Seminar, who recently likened the idea of Christ's resurrection to religious propaganda. At the least, resurrections were common occurrences in religious folklore.

24

The Ascension of Christ

The ascension of gods or great men represented their passage from a natural to a spiritual order. And since in mythology, the distant sky, or heaven, was seen as the abode of the gods, an ascent was necessarily an uplifting event.

Following his resurrection, the great god Osiris chose not to resume his earthly duties but, instead, ascended into heaven. Adonis also ascended into heaven in the presence of his Egyptian and Phoenician worshippers, and the ascent of Mithra's soul through the seven spheres was taught in the Mithraic mysteries. On the death of Attis, however, having turned into a pine tree, he was unable to ascend.

A number of saints were said to have been transported, while alive, to the world beyond the grave. Legend said that Enoch was carried by angels into heaven, where the Lord received him. Elijah was said to have been transported to heaven by a chariot of fire, successor to the legend that he was lifted to heaven in a whirlwind. Assumptions after death included that of Hercules, who was carried to heaven in a chariot drawn by four horses, the earth not being a suitable resting place for one so godlike. Similar reasoning resulted in the assumption of the Virgin Mary, which was announced by the Church in the seventh century.

One of the more compelling stories involved Moses, about whom it was said that God descended to earth to personally claim Moses's soul and escort him to heaven. They went up hand in hand.

It was probably to be expected, then, that Jesus was said to have ascended into heaven. An early depiction showed Jesus standing on a hill as the hand of God emerged from a cloud and drew him heavenward. Perhaps the last word on his ascension belongs to Joseph Campbell who, in a lecture, once noted that had Jesus ascended at the speed of light, he would not have cleared our own galaxy by the year 2000.

All in all, ascensions were a fitting end to lives that were said to be miraculous in every respect.

25

THE MYTHS OF CHRISTENDOM

In the ancient world, religious myth was the only available explanation for the world and its workings. Science had not yet come into its own, and it was religion that spoke to the basic concerns of human existence—questions about human origins, propensities, and the circumstance of death. And religion also spoke on questions concerning natural phenomena.

Religion responded to these questions by theorizing that invisible beings must be at work. It was an invisible-man theory of the universe wherein everything in nature was the work of activating spirits, and so awesome creatures filled the ancient skies. There were corn-goddesses with golden tresses, cow-headed gods of Egyptian origin, Greek gods of surpassing personal beauty, bull-gods with impressive sexual powers, feathered serpents with a taste for blood, warrior-gods with a lust for battle, storm-gods who controlled the elements, and many other notable flights of fancy.

When Christianity emerged as a fledgling religion, it adopted the belief in a spirit world and one of the ancient gods. And it drew its most fundamental beliefs from the mythologies of the older religions. Before Christianity's claim, the ancient world had counted many man-gods among its legendary figures, had provided for the forgiveness of sin, had proclaimed the efficacy of prayer, and had assured the faithful of an afterlife. The rites of communion, baptism, and exorcism were also the coinage of more ancient societies. So essentially, Christianity was not an original construct but more a collection of ancient ideologies.

The mythologist Joseph Campbell once noted that legends of virgins giving birth to godlike figures who die and are resurrected were commonplace in the Mediterranean and "furnished models to the early Christians for their representations of Christ." In fact, all the major events in the life of Christ—his heralded coming, virgin birth, divine nature, redemptive death, resurrection, and ascension—were events associated with mythical personages who preceded Christ and who appeared to have served as models for his miraculous existence.

On an ending note, Campbell had observed that the Aztecs, even before the Catholic Spaniards arrived, worshipped a high god, who was both remote and unbelievably powerful, together with "an incarnate Savior, associated with a serpent, born of a virgin, who had died and was resurrected, one of whose symbols was a cross." The Spanish padres reportedly viewed this as a "hideously degenerate form of their own revelation," in which the devil probably had a hand.

And perhaps, in part, that is what led Joseph Campbell to conclude, "The entire history on which our leading occidental religions have been founded is an anthology of fictions. But these are fictions of a type that have had—curiously enough—a universal vogue as the founding legends of other religions, too."

*   *   *

PART II

THE RIVALRY OF SCIENCE AND RELIGION

1

Introduction: In the Beginning

In recent years, there have been a number of theories put forward concerning the origin of the universe, some with intriguing names, such as the big bang theory. Still, the proofs are not in place for a definitive answer, and we content ourselves with the speculations of those who are knowledgeable in the field. We have advanced the cause somewhat, however, and may feel fairly certain that our forebears were wrong in attributing the creation of the universe to a large figure dressed in a flowing white robe. And yet that was, in fact, the concept of creation espoused by the Christian world for some two thousand years.

The Creator was perceived as a mighty figure of benign countenance, whose brow was furrowed and muscles knotted by his exertions. He was often shown in repose, weary after six days of creation, when in a heroic labor he had fashioned the universe. The moon and stars were literally hung from the firmament and the sun put on its course by his giant hand. In due time, the idea of a hands-on creation evolved into a more impressive concept still—that the universe was formed simply by a *word,* as in "He spake and they were made."

The time span allotted to the Almighty's creative process was befittingly brief, although the estimate did suffer from an apparent contradiction. One account of Genesis spoke of the six days of Creation, each with a morning and an evening, and a daily record of accomplishment. The second account of Genesis spoke of a single day only with Creation as an instantaneous act. This disparity was later resolved by St. Augustine and St. Thomas Aquinas who distinguished between the creation of substance (done in a single moment) and the separating, shaping, and styling considerations that consumed the remainder of the six days.

Ultimately, the six days of Creation led to the establishment of a date when the world began. The first attempt came from the bishop of Antioch who, in the second century, concluded that the world began six thousand years before Christ; he had coupled the six days of Creation with another reference found in scripture: "One day is with the Lord as a thousand years," and thus six thousand years.[1]

The beginning date of Creation, however, was addressed with more certainty than the identity of the Creator; scripture offered varied insights into his person. Some theologians believed that the third person of the Trinity was the creative agent, but others found scriptural support for the first or second persons of the Trinity; still others thought the phrase in Genesis "Let us make" pointed to a joint effort. Reflections on this issue led to a variety of artistic representations, including a team comprised of both a youthful and venerable Creator. Some representations showed the Creator with a single body but three faces, not unlike the supreme being of India and other ancient deities.

This puzzlement was greatly eased when, beyond scripture, sacred art contributed to a visualization of God creating the universe. Andrew Dickson White suggests that the early ideas about Creation were greatly enhanced when, in 1512, Michelangelo created his frescoes for the Sistine Chapel. He had been commissioned by the pope, Julius II, and the majesty of his work filled the faithful with awe. White describes it as follows:

In the midst of the expanse of heaven the Almighty Father—the first person of the Trinity—in human form, august and venerable, attended by angels and upborne by mighty winds, sweeps over the abyss, and, moving through successive compartments of the great vault, accomplishes the work of the creative days. With a single gesture he divides the light from the darkness, rears on high the solid firmament, gathers together beneath it the seas, or summons into existence the sun, and planets, and sets them circling about the earth.[2]

Another representation of creation—perhaps less likely to glorify the medieval idea—was exhibited in 1894 on a banner that celebrated the four hundredth anniversary of the founding of the Munich Cathedral. Andrew Dickson White describes a German view of the creation of the world:

Jesus of Nazareth, as a beautiful boy and with a nimbus encircling his head, was shown turning and shaping the globe on a lathe, which he keeps in motion with his foot. The emblems of the Passion are about him, God the Father looking approvingly upon him from a cloud, and the dove hovering between the two.[3]

All the representations of Creation, for better or worse artistically, show the latitude available to the artist as he or she portrayed the origin of the universe. For example, a stained glass window in the Cathedral at Ulm depicted the creation of animals, in this case the Almighty fashioning an elephant that had just been dressed with armor, harness, and the accouterments of war. In still other representations, the Creator was shown as a "tailor, seated, needle in hand, diligently sewing together skins of beasts into coats for Adam and Eve."[4] Quite a number of representations of the Almighty chose to show only his hand, with lightning bolts issuing from his forefinger, or his thumb and forefinger being used to spin the earth as if it were a top. And none of the aforementioned representations gave offense to the faithful of the Middle Ages who were grateful for any insight into the creation of their world.

Threefold God

In a thirteenth century manuscript, the Christian godhead is depicted with three heads, representing the Father, Son, and Holy Spirit.

(St. John's College, Cambridge)

So the Christian church undertook to explain the universe, beginning with Creation itself and covering all the workings of the natural world. Earthquakes were held to be the voice of an angry god, rain was caused by angels opening the windows of heaven, the stars were hung in the sky each night by the Almighty, comets were flung across the sky to frighten the wicked, and the sound of church bells could ward off marauding demons. And were it not for a talking serpent meeting an overcurious Eve in a magic garden, there would be no toil or trouble, no disease or natural disasters, and human beings would live forever in a perfect world. Such was a sampling of Christian belief that lasted for many centuries.

Today, it may seem strange that our culture would have believed in talking snakes and the story of Creation as described in Genesis, and for the better part of two thousand years. And yet most of our forebears subscribed to what are now accepted by most scientists and many theologians as mythical tales taken from more primitive cultures and even prehistoric sources. In part, the explanation is in the confidence that Christians had in the literal truth of the Bible and also in the encouragement of such beliefs by the Church hierarchy. Then, too, no alternative explanations of the universe were available for people to consider.

Then, in the sixteenth century, or thereabouts, a new interest arose in science and its potential for explaining the natural world. And it was a cause of great concern to the Christian church when an upstart science began to topple many long-standing religious beliefs and threaten the authority of the Church.

Notes

1   Andrew Dickson White, *A History of the Warfare of Science with Theology in Christendom*, vol. 1 (New York: D. Appleton-Century, 1936), p. 250.

2   Ibid., p. 11.

3   Ibid., p. 12.

4   Ibid., p. 27.

2

SCIENCE: HOLD BACK THE DAWN

E ven before a formal scientific discipline existed, many ancient civilizations had advanced their knowledge of natural science to a remarkable degree through observation and simple trial and error. Some early civilizations were familiar enough with astronomy to be able to predict an eclipse centuries before the invention of the telescope or a comprehensive understanding of measures and mathematics. And so it appears that humans have always been interested in questions concerning the environment and the possibility of either adapting or altering the environment to their own advantage. Indeed, the success of every generation and culture may be measured by its contributions to understanding the universe and furthering the harmonious relationship of its parts. And perhaps that is a fair definition of what science is all about.

It seems evident, then, that science is a natural consequence of humans being thrust into a strange environment and, therefore, the question of why science, if it is so necessary and a natural a part of our existence, led a shadowy existence for the better part of the last two thousand years. The short answer is that the study of natural science was overwhelmed by speculations on the supernatural, particularly after the beginning of Christianity when all natural happenings were credited to a divine agency. Moreover, any consideration of science was unavailing because the truth about the universe was thought to be known through divine revelation; few people doubted that the Jewish and Christian holy books revealed as much about natural science as the Creator wished to have known. In view of this, people were concerned that their explorations of the natural world might be an encroachment on the realm of the supernatural. Socrates himself was said to have been concerned that investigations of certain physical phenomena were intrusions on the province of a divine authority.

And then there was the futility of exploring a world that was about to end. In what may now be recognized as a recurring theme, theologians taught that the world was doomed and that the day of judgment was fast approaching. Consequently, it was foolish for humans to ponder this world when their days would be better spent preparing for the life to come. It was a convincing argument at the time and made investigations into natural phenomena seem a futile, if not a frivolous, pursuit. So the end of the world was near, and all attention was focused on hopes for an eternal existence rather than the world at hand.

Even the presumed end of the world, however, did not altogether close down the curiosity of humans about their environment. But now another reason for the dormancy of science emerged: the Church had of necessity made rather elaborate explanations of natural phenomena and did not welcome any new truths from outside the Church—and particularly if the new truths were in conflict with the old. So any scientific findings were obliged to confirm the existing truth as defined by scripture and its interpretation by theologians, particularly those dealing with Creation. Of course the accounts of Creation shown in scripture were simply a collection of myths and legends that, as Andrew Dickson White notes, were "largely derived by the Hebrews from their ancient relations with Chaldea, re-wrought in a monotheistic sense,

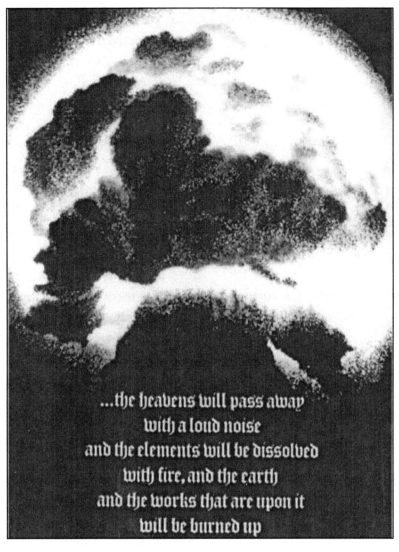

...the heavens will pass away
with a loud noise
and the elements will be dissolved
with fire, and the earth
and the works that are upon it
will be burned up

A Doomed World

Religions of the world, including Christianity, have often taught
that the world was doomed—a powerful incentive to keep the faith.

(Camera Press Ltd., London)

imperfectly welded together, and then thrown into poetic forms in the sacred books which we have inherited."[1] Nevertheless, it was to these scriptural truths that scientific findings were obliged to conform.

Actually, the need for science to conform to existing beliefs went beyond scripture. For thousands of years, a body of religious beliefs had been building all by way of explaining and controlling natural phenomena. Some beliefs came from scripture, others came from letters, discourses, myths; still others came from pagan superstitions that were found to provide a convenient link between the old beliefs and the new teachings of Christianity. At the discretion of the church fathers, these ancient beliefs were accepted as sacred, and once defined as sacred, they became unassailable.

So it was that any scientific finding, or hypothesis, was first tested for its compatibility with Christian dogma—and here, the screen was exceedingly fine. Theology was considered infinitely superior to science based on the presumption of its divine origin; as a result, any controversy was resolved in favor of the religious belief. It came down to the fact that science was to be used (if at all) to confirm the teachings of the Church, certainly not to refute them. And the authority of the Church was used to nip any possible source of controversy in the bud.

An unfortunate example of the Church's authority took place in Alexandria, a great center of learning at the beginning of the fifth century. It was there that a Greek philosopher named Hypatia attracted the wealthy and fashionable of Alexandria by her discourses on the doctrines of Plato and Aristotle as well as her comments on matters of science. But her discourses were objected to by the bishopric of Alexandria, St. Cyril, and this confrontation of science and religion was to end unhappily for Hypatia: "As Hypatia retired to her academy, she was assaulted by Cyril's mob—a mob of many monks. Stripped naked in the street, she was dragged into a church and there killed by the club of Peter the Reader. The corpse was cut to pieces, the flesh was scraped from the bones with shells, and the remnants cast into a fire. For this frightful crime Cyril was never called to account. It seemed that the end sanctified the means."[2] This marked the end of Greek philosophy in Alexandria and served as a warning to those who would promote thought that ran counter to the teachings of Christianity.

In the early centuries, as well, religion maintained its position that truth and knowledge were to be found only in holy scripture, and church leaders provided a number of interesting ways to resolve any controversies. Ordeal tribunals made their appearance, whereby persons accused of heresy were judged by being thrown into lakes; the innocent swam to shore and the guilty drowned. Similarly, those who could hold red-hot irons in their hands without being burnt were deemed innocent as were those who could keep their arms outstretched like a cross for a longer period than their accuser.

In the twelfth century, a tide of new learning and belief appeared, together with more than a suspicion that the bishop of Rome was not the supreme lord of the universe and that Church doctrine was, to a significant extent, a compilation of error and superstition. The papal government answered with two institutions: the requirement of auricular (personal) confession to a priest, thought by some to be the means of detecting heretics, and the Inquisition, which—over a three-hundred-year period—punished 340,000 persons, according to reports, with almost 32,000 of these burned alive. And the Church formalized its restraint on science:

- In 1163, Pope Alexander III forbade "the study of physics or the laws of the world" to all ecclesiastics who, at the time, were the only people in a position to attempt such studies.

- In 1243, the Dominicans forbade members of the order the study of medicine and natural philosophy and, in 1287, extended the prohibition to the study of chemistry.

- In 1317, Pope John XXII issued his bull *Spondent Pariter*, which was aimed at alchemists but also hit the beginning studies of chemistry.

And then in 1559, Pope Paul IV brought forth the Congregation of the Index Expurgatorius, whose duty it was to examine books that were then becoming widely available through the invention of the printing press. At first, the Congregation simply identified books that people were forbidden to read, but later, prohibitions were imposed on publishing the books. Although rivals, Catholics and Protestants agreed on the need to suppress learning that was not consistent with scripture.

By now, however, even in its own ranks, the Church was confronted with ideas that ran counter to its teachings on such subjects as transubstantiation, the immaculate conception, and the plurality of worlds. One such dissenter was Giordano Bruno, an Italian who was born only seven years after the death of Copernicus and who began his career as a member of the Dominican order. Among his writings was a rejection of the idea that the earth was flat and functioned as the center of the universe. For this he was imprisoned, tried, and found guilty; and on his refusal to recant, was sentenced by Pope Clement VIII to be punished "as mercifully as possible and without the shedding of blood," which is to say burned alive. His last words perhaps reflect the fear and hysteria that, in 1600, attended religious dissent: "Perhaps it is with greater fear that you pass the sentence upon me than I receive it."

So the Christian church felt justified in restraining scientific thought by whatever means necessary in order to preserve its traditional beliefs. Curiously, torture was not inconsistent with Christian beliefs because

God himself was thought to have sentenced millions of people to fiery furnaces for an eternity. In effect, then, the Church found in the supposed character of God its justification for imposing punishments and death on those who dared to challenge its sacred beliefs.

Notes

[1] Andrew Dickson White, *A History of the Warfare of Science with Theology in Christendom*, vol. 1 (New York: D. Appleton-Century, 1936), p. 22.

[2] John William Draper, *History of the Conflict between Religion and Science* (New York: D. Appleton, 1902), p. 55.

3

SCIENCE AND THE SORCERER'S ART

Another reason why science was slow in developing during the Middle Ages was an unfortunate confusion between science and magic. The Church saw a danger in the practice of magic and parallels between magic and science, which led religious authorities to suspect and often persecute the practitioners of both.

And in fact, magic was similar to science in that neither technique called on invisible spirits. Both were based on the assumption of a natural law and the belief that a given action would produce a predictable reaction. For example, just as a scientist might seed the clouds, so did the ancient magician sprinkle water on the ground in order to produce rain.

Both magic and science, then, attempted to control the forces of nature by using nature's own laws. Their development, however, was quite independent of each other, and in later days, the patently false premises of magic led it to become known as the "bastard sister of science."

Early Magic

Early peoples came to believe in magic based on their own observations of natural phenomena from which they drew two conclusions: first, that in nature, the effect usually resembles the cause, or "like produces like" (imitative magic); and second, that the parts of a body may affect the whole, even when separated by time and space (contagious magic). Both the imitative and contagious types became known as sympathetic magic, as they recognized an affinity or interdependence of natural phenomena.

Imitative magic took many forms. One example is the case of a medicine man drawing the yellow jaundice from a patient by placing a yellow bird in his close proximity. Certain warriors around the world would not eat rabbit, believing that they might imitate the rabbit and develop a timid personality—for the same reason, some tribes ate the meat of lions to develop a fearless character. Even the gods were chosen based on their perceived relation to the function performed; thus bulls or snakes were often worshipped as fertility gods and a yellow-haired goddess represented the corn crop.

Contagious magic was equally powerful in the mind of many early peoples. A magician could obtain a lock of hair from an enemy and, by destroying the detached hair, destroy the enemy—without regard to the time or space that separated the magician from his victim. For this reason, some tribes never cut their hair, and some influentials paid retainers to eat their hair and nail clippings so they could not be appropriated by an enemy. Names were also carefully guarded in many early societies and fake identities given so that magicians could not aim their curses with any degree of accuracy.

As early tribal societies developed, magic remained an important element for controlling human affairs and often blended with a belief in a spirit world. The Jews, for example, combined magic and religion in such a way as to maximize their utility. The Jewish religion acknowledged the existence of demons, a religious concept, but then used magic to harness their demonic powers. Such was the case when, in legend, Solomon used evil spirits—demons—to assist in building the Temple in Jerusalem.[1]

Other ancient civilizations, including the Egyptian and later the Greek and Roman, showed few substantive differences between their religious beliefs and magic. For the most part, religious beliefs were simply those beliefs that the state had accepted as the conventional wisdom while the less orthodox beliefs tended to be classed as magic. The difference was one of convention, not kind. And in the fullness of time, many magical rites became an accepted part of religious ceremonies.

Roman Magic

Rome, the cradle of Christianity, was home to many of the earlier beliefs concerning magic and the power of magicians. As in earlier cultures, Romans wore amulets to protect themselves against magic spells and marauding demons. They leveled curses at their enemies and made small figures from wax or clay with which they could cast magic spells on victims who were far removed. Another manifestation of their belief in sympathetic magic was the popular belief that jaundice could be transferred from a human to other living things that were colored yellow.

Magic in ancient Rome served many of the same purposes as religion, such as healing the sick, controlling inclement weather, assuring the harvest, restoring virility, and increasing sexual desire. And magic also shared many of the same costumes used in religion, such as a flowing white robe often adorned with purple streamers. Purification rites, as well, were often used in both magical and religious ceremonies.

A Demon King

Magicians claimed the ability to conjure up demons, this one a bearded king riding on a long-tailed dragon.

(From an 1801 text, British Museum/Michael Holford)

The greatest of all magicians was also a goddess, Hecate, queen of ghosts, whose powers were universal, but whose special talents centered on the magic of love and metamorphosis. A daunting figure, she was often seen sweeping through the night sky followed by her train of questing spirits.

Christianity and Magic

In the fourth century, therefore, when Christ was designated a man-god and Christianity became the state religion of the Roman Empire, sympathetic magic was still believed in by most Romans. A Roman magician could bring the dead to life if he possessed a bone belonging to the departed or magically effect a transfer of jaundice from the body of a patient to that of a yellow bird. Romans also assumed that the poor productivity of their own wheat field, while their neighbor's field blossomed, was the result of a magical transference of their crop.

So Romans continued to believe in the real power of magic and held that any differences between their Christian religion and magic might be a difference between good and evil, but that it was not a difference between the real and imaginary. St. Augustine, for example, was satisfied that magical rites could be used to summon demons from the netherworld.

As Christianity spread, it was to have many confrontations with the magic of foreign lands. During his time in Ireland, for example, St. Patrick voiced his concern with the powerful magic of the Celtic women. And in fact, Ireland became a battleground of sorts where the magic of the Christian saints was pitted against that of the evil druids. Each party was thought capable of changing shape, becoming invisible, producing food miraculously, and leveling an opponent with the power of its curses. In this case, the Church again acknowledged its belief in the power of magic, whether wrought by its own priests or the priests of other persuasions.

Finally, however, the Church concluded that magic of any sort should be classed as Satanic in origin, presumably the work of dethroned pagan gods who worked to overthrow the Church.

Thus defined, the Church went to great lengths to ban the practice of magic that, unfortunately, had by then become somewhat confused with science, which prompted the papacy to move against both:

- In 1163, Pope Alexander III forbade "the study of physics or the laws of the world" to all ecclesiastics who, at the time, were the only people in a position to attempt such studies.

- In 1231, Pope Gregory IX instituted the papal Inquisition to seek out heretics practicing alchemy, witchcraft and sorcery (the use of torture to obtain confessions was authorized in 1252 by Innocent IV).

- In 1243, the Dominicans forbade members of the order the study of medicine and natural philosophy and, in 1287, extended the prohibition to the study of chemistry.

- In 1317, Pope John XXII issued his bull *Spondent Pariter*, which was aimed at alchemists but also hit the beginning studies of chemistry. Pope John noted that the lives of he and his followers were threatened by the arts of sorcerers who sent devils into mirrors, killed people with a magic word, and had tried to kill him by piercing a waxen image of himself.

- In 1437 and 1445, Pope Eugene IV issued bulls encouraging inquisitors to seek out and punish magicians and witches who produce inclement weather.

- In 1484, Pope Innocent VIII issued his bull *Summis Desiderantes*, which caused the death of tens of thousands of men, women, and children suspected of sorcery and magic. About this time, the

Church published the witch-hammer, *Malleus Maleficarum*, which was a manual detailing the means of detecting and punishing witches.

• The years 1504 and 1523 saw Pope Julius II and Pope Adrian VI issue similar bulls condemning magicians and witches.

Witches on High

For centuries, the Christian fathers believed in the existence of witches who, as agents of Satan, were thought to conspire against the Church.

(Dover Publications)

Over the centuries, therefore, the Church documented its belief in the real power of magic by a series of written proclamations and by the persecution of those suspected of witchcraft or sorcery. Ironically, however, many elements of sympathetic magic had already found their way into religious beliefs and remain there today. For example, today's belief that body parts of the dead, when preserved, have powers to protect the living was born in the sympathetic magic of early tribal societies.

The fact that the Church recognized magic as a real event necessarily acted as another damper on scientific studies, for if events in the world could be controlled by magic (or religion), there was nothing to be gained by science and its inquiries into cause and effect. And there was a growing concern among the church fathers that science was a threatening process that had the potential to refute many of Christianity's long-standing beliefs—in short, a devilish pursuit.

The end result was that science remained in the doldrums for well over a thousand years. Not until the sixteenth century did science regain any sense of momentum—and when it did, it was because science adopted a method that would offer proof of its findings.

Notes

[1] James Hastings, ed., "Magic," *The Encyclopaedia of Religion and Ethics* (New York: Charles Scribner and Sons, 1951), p. 303.

4

SCIENTIFIC METHOD: A NEW BEGINNING

Religion and magic both began when humans first observed the world around them and tried to determine the causes of natural phenomena and then to exercise some measure of control over them. But neither priest nor sorcerer could, in any way, prove the efficacy of their undertakings.

Certainly, magic could not confirm its ability to still the tempest, confound the enemy, raise the dead, or save the crops. Nor had religion demonstrated an ability to achieve these ends by the invocation of spirits. Both asked their adherents to accept their powers on faith; their failures were then attributed to the opposition of unseen forces (other sorcerers or evil spirits) or perhaps to punishable flaws in the characters of their adherents (who presumably were not worthy of help). To the extent that these explanations were accepted by the faithful, the magicians and priests persevered, the rituals were repeated, and the beliefs were perpetuated.

Science was little better in the beginning but was saved by an inevitable evolution: rational thinking took the place of the wishful thinking that had characterized magic and religion. And the simple trial and error of science developed into a true scientific method. Progress was a gradual affair and, like most human endeavors, was helped along by countless people, but there were two men who marked the beginning of this new outlook and approach to science: Roger Bacon (c. 1220-1292) and Francis Bacon (1561-1626).

Both Roger Bacon and Francis Bacon were inventive individuals. Roger Bacon sketched an airplane with flapping wings two centuries before Leonardo da Vinci made a similar drawing. Francis Bacon was the first person to note, from a map, that the continent of Africa appeared to have once been connected to South America. (Theologians at the time went on to surmise that the great deluge had pulled the two continents apart.)

Roger Bacon—Doctor Mirabilis

Roger Bacon was the first real advocate for experimentation as the basis for scientific conclusions, and in this respect, he led the field by some three hundred years. For this contribution, he is often regarded as the forerunner of the modern scientific method.

Roger Bacon was born in England of wealthy parents, who saw him schooled in mathematics, astronomy, optics, alchemy as well as languages. In the earlier part of his career, he devoted himself to lecturing on Aristotelian treatises and gave no indication of a consuming interest in science. But in 1247, he resigned his chair in the faculty of arts and became deeply involved in science, with a particular emphasis on experimental research. In the pursuit of his experiments, he established a small laboratory and is said to have spent great sums of money in designing instruments and training assistants in the work at hand. The work covered a broad spectrum of chemistry and physics—the *New Encyclopedia Britannica* notes, "He seriously studied the problem of flying in a machine with flapping wings. He was the first person in the West to give exact directions for making gunpowder ... Bacon described spectacles [which also soon came into use]; elucidated the principles of reflection, refraction, and spherical aberration; and proposed mechanically propelled ships and carriages. He used a camera obscura [which projects an image through a pinhole] to observe eclipses of the sun."

Perhaps Bacon's best-known work relates to his studies on the nature of light and on the causes and character of the rainbow. Until his explanation of the rainbow, the world believed the legend found in the book of Genesis wherein the Holy Spirit caused a "bow in the cloud" as a sign to mortals that there would not be another deluge.

In 1257, Roger Bacon made another abrupt change of lifestyle and joined the Franciscan order of Friars Minor, but in a short time, he was severely disciplined by his superiors for his experiments and outspoken interest in science.

In 1266, Bacon appealed to Pope Clement IV with a proposal that the curricula of major universities be expanded to include comprehensive courses in science. In the following two years, and at the request of the Pope, Bacon completed what amounted to an encyclopedia of science—the more remarkable because a papal order of secrecy prevented his seeking approval for the project from his Order. However, Pope Clement died in 1268, and Bacon's proposal went no further.

The story of Roger Bacon ends with his imprisonment in 1278, the result of being condemned by his fellow Franciscans. St. Bonaventura had silenced him, Jerome of Ascoli (later Pope) then imprisoned him on charges of "dangerous novelties" and the suspicion of sorcery. He remained in prison for fourteen years and was near eighty years of age when he was released. His last work was not completed when he died in 1292. Bacon's contribution to science was notable in a number of areas, particularly optics, but he will be remembered for his insistence on experimentation to determine the true nature of things. His efforts in this direction earned him the name Doctor Mirabilis, "Wonderful Teacher."

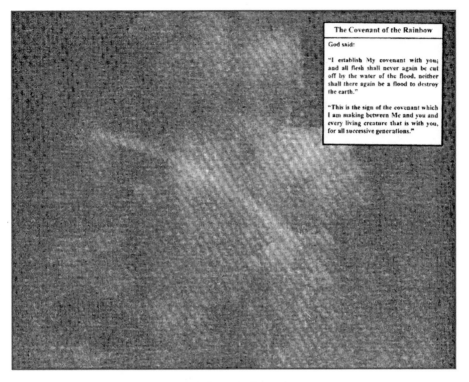

The Covenant of the Rainbow

God said:

"I establish My covenant with you; and all flesh shall never again be cut off by the water of the flood, neither shall there again be a flood to destroy the earth."

"This is the sign of the covenant which I am making between Me and you and every living creature that is with you, for all successive generations."

A Rainbow's Promise

Christians believed that the rainbow was a sign that God would never again destroy the earth by flood. Many cultures had similar beliefs about rainbows.

(Dembinski Photo Associates)

Francis Bacon—A New Method

Of equal importance in developing a scientific method was Francis Bacon, aptly described as a man for all seasons. Bacon first attended Trinity College, Cambridge, with the intention of becoming a diplomat. Soon after, he was admitted to Gray's Inn where he studied law, became a barrister in 1582, lord chancellor and baron in 1618, and viscount in 1620/21.

Along the way, Francis Bacon developed an abiding interest in the philosophy of science. His celebrated work *Novum Organon* (*New Instrument*) was published in 1620 and openly challenged the involvement of theology in scientific affairs. He questioned those who would base their natural philosophy on the books of Genesis and Job and other sacred scriptures and suspected that theologians sometimes repressed science so that things could be referred more easily to the hand of God.

Andrew White credits Bacon with establishing science as an independent discipline: "The *Novum Organon*, considering the time when it came from his pen, is doubtless one of the greatest exhibitions of genius in the history of human thought. It showed the modern world the way out of the scholastic method and reverence for dogma into the experimental method and reverence for fact. In it occur many passages which show that the great philosopher was fully alive to the danger both to religion and to science arising from their mixture."[1]

But Francis Bacon's vision went well beyond considerations of religion to the point of establishing the basis for a true scientific method although, as often happens in science, the Baconian method was later found wanting in some respects because the exhaustive—even endless—cataloguing of facts inhibited the imagination and promised no end to an investigation. Today, the creative use of hypotheses serves these purposes.

Overall, a scientific method rests at the opposite end of an acceptance based on faith. While those who believe in magic must simply accept the premise that the magical rite will work to achieve the desired end result, and those who believe in religion must satisfy themselves that spirits exist based on hearsay, science, and a scientific method offers some proof of cause and effect.

Notes

[1] Andrew Dickson White, *A History of the Warfare of Science with Theology in Christendom*, vol. 1 (New York: D. Appleton-Century, 1936), p. 400.

5

ASTRONOMY AND THE HAND OF GOD

E arly humans must have gazed into the heavens, ever enthralled by the splendid show of natural phenomena. The sun traveled across the sky and, from above, gave light and heat to the world below. Rain fell from the heavens to nourish various life-forms, and snow dropped its coverlet of white. Storms were born in the sky where thunder sounded and lightning played. And the moon and stars brightened the darkness of the night. Early humans reacted to such wonders by supposing that gods—invisible spirits—controlled such events, and indeed, there was no other explanation available at the time.

Of course, the earth was nevertheless thought to be at the center of things because that is where humankind lived, and we have always been disposed to think of ourselves as center stage in the drama of the universe. And so it was that, for many centuries, religion was wedded to the idea that the earth was the center of our planetary system—the geocentric theory. Not only had the geocentric theory been supported by such an eminent astronomer as Ptolemy (AD 100-165), but the theory was totally consistent with the Church's presumption that the earth was the center of the universe and humankind the center of life on earth.

The other planets were regarded in various ways. Some fathers of the Church, such as Origen (c. 185-254), believed that heavenly bodies were living things and possessed souls. Other fathers believed that angels inhabited the stars and moved them about, while still other theologians believed that stars were used by angels as omens.

Overall, the Church's earliest view of the heavens was that of a solid firmament above the earth on whose ceiling the heavenly bodies were hung as lights, certainly for functional purposes, but perhaps for decor as well. St. Philastrius (fourth century), in his famous treatise, pronounced it a heresy to deny that the stars were brought out by God from his treasure-house and hung in the sky each evening; any other view he declared false to the Catholic faith.

In the sixth century, Cosmas again explained the universe based on scripture and envisioned the universe as an oblong box; planetary movement was the work of angels who had been appointed for that purpose. So also were the "windows of heaven" opened and shut by winged creatures, and all was well in a universe ordered by the angels.

Then from about the ninth century through the thirteenth century, several prominent theologians refined the Church's concept of the universe, culminating with St. Thomas Aquinas, the Angelic Doctor (1225-1274), who fully developed a sacred theory of the universe. By now, the earth was no longer conceived as flat and the universe as an oblong box. Instead, the earth and the planets had become globes, encircled by transparent spheres that were rotated by angels. One of the spheres was the empyrean, which contained all the other spheres and in which God sat enthroned.

This entire universe, ruled by the Divine Majesty, was activated and administered by a vast organization of angels, divided into hierarchies and orders that we know as follows:

- The seraphim, cherubim, and thrones, who continually chanted divine praises.

- The order of dominions, powers, and empire, who received divine commands activated the sun, moon, and planets; and guarded their brethren.

- The principalities, archangels, and angels, who controlled the nations, religion, and the general run of earthly affairs.

And finally, there were the rebellious angels who not only troubled the good angels but were also responsible for inclement weather: thunder and lightning, heat waves and hail. St. Thomas Aquinas supposed that adverse atmospheric conditions were permitted as disciplinary measures and possibly represented a deserved punishment for sin.

So from the second to the sixteenth century, the nature of the universe was decided by an interpretation of the scriptures, and any issues were resolved by the fathers of the Church. All knowledge was held to be included in the Old and New Testaments, and other ideas were regarded as profane. John Draper noted that the preference for sacred over profane learning was so great that "Christianity had been in existence fifteen hundred years and had not produced a single astronomer."[1]

And while the Muhammadan nations were making great strides in understanding the universe, Christendom's attention centered on image worship, transubstantiation, miracles, shrine cures, and the wondrous lives of the saints.

The World Turns

When the rotation of the earth was at last acknowledged by the Church,
it was believed that angels were the instruments of its revolution.

(Illustration from *The Way Things Work* by David Macaulay)

On Signs and Wonders

As our ancestors in the ancient world believed that God had made
the earth for men and women and had given us the sun and moon
to light our way, it followed that all heavenly phenomena would be
attributed to the same source. And so from a heavenly throne, the

Almighty would hang the stars out at night, cast forth lightning to frighten the wicked, and display signs and wonders for an earthbound audience. In the ancient world, every heavenly happening was searched for significance, and comets gave the ancients ample food for thought.

Andrew Dickson White noted the widespread belief that stars and meteors presaged happy events, "especially the births of gods, heroes and great men."[2] It even became an unspoken tradition for godlike figures to first appear on earth amidst or announced by heavenly lights. The sacred books of India recount that the births of Krishna and Buddha were announced by heavenly lights. In China, sacred books noted the appearance of heavenly lights before the birth of Yu, the founder of the first dynasty, and also of the wise man, Lao-tzu. Jewish legend has a star appearing before the birth of Moses, and when Abraham was born, the occasion was marked by a new star in the east. The tradition of heavenly lights was found in Greek and Roman legend as well, such as in the birth of various Caesars. And of course, the sacred books of Christianity report that a star, rising in the east, heralded the coming of Christ.

All in all, then, religions often chose to associate the coming of their godlike figures with stars and meteors, which provided a poetic accompaniment to their appearance and a direct connection between them and their creator, the ruler of the universe.

As heavenly lights presage happy events, so did eclipses foretell tragedy or the disappointment of a divine being with his people below. The Greeks believed that darkness befell the earth on the death of Prometheus, Hercules, and Alexander the Great. The Romans believed the world was dark for six hours at the death of Romulus, and the lights went out again when Julius Caesar died. One of the Christian legends surrounding the Crucifixion reported six to nine hours of darkness over the globe, and Jewish tradition noted a three-day period of darkness when the books of the law were translated into Greek—a profanity. And the story is that, in Massachusetts, a gentleman named Increase Mather thought an eclipse was evidence that nature grieved over the death of President Chauncey of Harvard College.

Generally, science had little quarrel with religion's idea that the coming of great men was presaged by heavenly lights and their going accompanied by a global darkness. There was no harm done by such beliefs.

Comets, however, represented a more serious question. Now, a few of the ancient peoples regarded comets as harmless, and Seneca (c. 4 BC-AD 65), alone among the ancients, surmised that comets might move in accordance with fixed laws of nature. But the majority of people believed that comets were fireballs tossed around the heavens by an angry god. The early fathers of the Church believed this; and such theologians as Origen in the third century, the Venerable Bede in the eighth century, St. Thomas Aquinas in the thirteenth century, and Martin Luther in the sixteenth century were unanimous in their opinion that comets were divine warnings to humanity and portents of calamities to come.

One ecclesiastic found no fewer than eighty-six biblical texts that signaled the Almighty's intention to use heavenly bodies as the means to instruct humans on future events—after analyzing the times and plans of comets, he published under the title *The Comet Hour-Book*. In effect, it described everything one might want to know about comets and the significance of their appearance. Unhappily, he concluded that in all such appearances, comets represented "messengers of misfortune."

The sacred science of the Middle Ages formed many opinions about comets, including their form, color, and content. In the opinion of one Celichius, a Lutheran bishop in 1578, the vapor surrounding a comet was "the thick smoke of human sins, rising every day, every hour, every moment, full of stench and horror, before the face of God, and becoming gradually so thick as to form a comet, with curled and plaited tresses, which at last is kindled by the hot and fiery anger of the Supreme Heavenly Judge."[3]

Another theologian gave special attention to the configuration of comets and recognized the shape of a trumpet in one, a spear in another, and subsequently, the shape of a goat, a torch, a sword, an arrow, and a bare arm. And from these shapes, it was possible to divine the intent of the Almighty in his fearful display. Again, the prevailing opinion was that comets portended nothing but bad news from above and that, more often than not, the people on earth were being punished for unthankfulness, voluptuousness, licentiousness, and perhaps, an inappropriate mode of dress.

There were also, White notes, frequent literary allusions to the significance of comets. Shakespeare makes the Duke of Bedford, lamenting at the bier of Henry V, say,

> Comets, importing change of time and states,Brandish your crystal tresses in the sky; And with them scourge the bad revolting stars, That have consented unto Henry's death.

Milton, speaking of Satan preparing for combat, says,

> On the other side, Incensed with indignation, Satan stood Unterrified, and like a comet burned, That fires the length of Ophiuchus huge In the arctic sky, and from its horrid hair Shakes pestilence and war.[4]

And Dante, in his *Divine Comedy*, had a vision of comets that was consistent with the religious thought of the time. When Satan was dismissed from heaven for his disobedience, he took the form of a flaming comet and plunged through the sky, striking the earth with such force that he opened up a hole to the center of the earth—which became hell.

Once again, a religious significance was being attributed to a natural happening. It followed that, as science developed hypotheses to explain the behavior of comets, religion resented the encroachment on its sacred beliefs.

The clergy took the position that scientific speculation was ungodly. Martin Luther (1483-1546), for example, said in one of his sermons, "The Heathen write that the comet may arise from natural causes, but God creates not one that does not foretoken a sure calamity."[5] Before the issue was resolved, the belief that comets were the instruments of a divine discontent struck terror to the hearts of people throughout the Middle Ages and, in doing so, strengthened the position of the Church who alone possessed the power and the knowledge to deal with God's great wrath.

Tycho Brahe (1546-1601) and Kepler (1571-1630) first proved that comets lay beyond the orbit of the moon and therefore were among the heavenly bodies that move in regular patterns. And in the seventeenth century, arguments against the superstitions surrounding comets began to appear in the works of such men as Balthasar Bekker (1634-1698) and then Pierre Bayle (1647-1706) who declared, "Comets are bodies subject to the ordinary law of Nature, and not prodigies amenable to no law."[6]

By now, scientific hypotheses and proofs were regularly assaulting the religious concept of comets, and the final proof came in 1682 when Halley recognized the comet as one which appeared at regular intervals—and foretold its return in about seventy-five years. The prediction came true, and as a result, comets came to be regarded as natural phenomena, explainable by natural law, contrary to the explanation offered by the Church. It followed that other astronomical events would no longer be viewed as a show-and-tell orchestrated by the Almighty.

Notes

1   John William Draper, *History of the Conflict between Religion and Science* (New York: D. Appleton, 1922), p. 158.

2   Andrew Dickson White, *A History of the Warfare of Science with Theology in Christendom*, vol. 1 (New York: D. Appleton-Century, 1936), p. 171.

3   Ibid., p. 190.

4   Ibid., p. 181.

5   Ibid., p. 182.

6   Ibid., p. 199.

6

ASTRONOMY: COPERNICUS AND GALILEO

There are few scientists who have so changed our concept of the universe as Copernicus and Galileo. Their work established the heliocentric theory of the universe and their lives have become well-known examples of the repression that the Christian hierarchy brought to bear on the free expression of scientific theories.

They were not the first men ever to consider the heliocentric theory. An alternative theory of the universe had been taking shape for a number of centuries. Pythagoras, in the sixth century BC, had suggested that the earth and other planets might revolve around the sun. The same theory was restated three centuries later by Aristarchus, who was promptly rewarded with a charge of blasphemy—this in the pre-Christian era. Martianus Capella voiced the heliocentric theory in the fifth century AD, and it was expressed again in the writings of Cardinal Nicholas de Cusa a thousand years later.

Then in the sixteenth century, along came Copernicus (1473-1543) with his hypothesis that the sun and planets do not revolve around the earth—quite the reverse, the earth and planets revolve around the sun. Nicholas Copernicus lived in a little town in Poland before going to Rome in AD 1500 where he was a professor. His theory was first mentioned in Rome, but only as a theory, given the probability that the papal court would frown on a more definite pronouncement. In fact, it was this consideration that led Copernicus to return to his town in Poland where, for thirty years, he nursed his idea and discussed it in private with friends.

When Copernicus finally determined to publish his landmark work *Revolutions of the Heavenly Bodies* in 1543, he dedicated it to the pope in the hope that this would smooth the way, and his friend Osiander wrote a preface that excused Copernicus by pronouncing the work a hypothesis and not a statement of fact. The finished book was delivered to Copernicus on his deathbed, and in a matter of hours, he had passed away—he was thus spared the controversy that was to come when even to read the work of Copernicus was to risk damnation.

At that time, both Catholic and Protestant authorities condemned the concept of a revolving earth. Martin Luther (1483-1546) said, "People gave ear to an upstart astrologer who strove to show that the earth revolves, not the heavens or the firmament, the sun and the moon. Whoever wishes to appear clever must devise some new system, which of all systems is of course the very best. This fool wishes to reverse the entire science of astronomy; but sacred scripture tells us that Joshua commanded the sun to stand still, and not the earth."[1] Other Protestant leaders used numerous scriptural texts to prove that the earth stands still in the center of the universe, contrary to the doctrine of Copernicus.

- Melanchthon, in his treatise *The Elements of Physics,* said, "Now, it is a want of honesty and decency to assert such notions publicly . . . it is the part of a good mind to accept the truth as revealed by God and to acquiesce in it."

Nicolaus Copernicus

The heliocentric theory of Copernicus challenged the Church's doctrine that the earth was the center of the universe—to believe otherwise was heresy.

(North Wind Picture Archives)

- Calvin, in his *Commentary of Genesis*, condemned all who agreed with Copernicus: "Who will venture to place the authority of Copernicus above that of the Holy Spirit?"

- John Wesley, also acknowledged that the ideas put forward by Copernicus "tend toward infidelity."[2]

One might suppose that the question of whether the sun revolves around the earth, or the earth around the sun, could have been a matter of indifference to the religious in the sixteenth century. But in fact, the religious leaders assumed that since the Copernican doctrine was clearly at odds with scripture, the doctrine must be viewed not as novelty but as heresy and those who subscribed to the doctrine punished. And it was more than a challenge to the accuracy of the scriptures—there were inferential considerations. If the earth was not the center of the universe and was indeed subordinate to other planets, this reflected on the power and majesty of its Creator.

The tomb of Copernicus carried the prayer: "I ask not the grace accorded to Paul; not that given to Peter; give me only the favor which Thou didst show to the thief on the cross." So his life ended as it had been lived—in a pious Christian manner. Nevertheless, in 1829, almost three hundred years after his death in 1543, no priest could be induced to conduct a memorial service for a multitude of people who had gathered at a church in Warsaw to honor Copernicus and unveil a statue to his memory. It was 1835, with the approval of Pius VII, before the works of Copernicus were removed from the Roman Catholic Index.

Galileo and the Inquisition

It was Galileo (1564-1642) who reaped the whirlwind when his discoveries with the telescope absolutely confirmed the doctrine of

Galileo Galilei

For his support of the Copernicus doctrine, Galileo was summoned before the Inquisition in Rome and forced to recant on pain of imprisonment or death.

(Roto Marburg/Art Resource, New York)

Copernicus. The telescope was invented in 1608 by a Hollander named Lippershey who found that distant objects could be magnified when two glass lenses were combined in a certain way. The next year Galileo heard of the invention and fashioned his own telescope and, over time, improved its power until it could magnify thirty times. Already a distinguished mathematician and scientist, Galileo proceeded to observe the heavens with his telescope and saw valleys and mountains on the moon, myriads of stars where there were thought to be none, and a formation of stars revolving around Jupiter that were, in miniature, a representation of the Copernican system.

With these and other discoveries, it was not long before Galileo was summoned before the Holy Inquisition and charged with heresy. The Church demanded that he recant and refrain from any further statements in support of the Copernican doctrine—and he did for sixteen years, under threat of imprisonment and with the knowledge that, in 1600, Giordano Bruno, an Italian philosopher, had been gagged and burned alive for his theory on the plurality of planets. The Church proceeded to silence any further discussion on Galileo's discoveries and forbade any further writings. The pope, said to be infallible in such matters, signed a bill condemning the Copernican concept, and throughout Europe, there appeared a flood of theological refutations of the Copernican doctrine. Typical of the arguments were those of Scipio Chiaramonti, dedicated to Cardinal Barberini: "Animals, which move, have limbs and muscles; the earth has no limbs or muscles, therefore it does not move. It is angels who make Saturn, Jupiter, the sun, etc., turn round. If the earth revolves, it must also have an angel in the centre to get it in motion; but only devils live there; it would therefore be a devil who would impart motion to the earth."[3]

Although Galileo had been quiet for sixteen years, he pursued his studies and, in 1632, published his work *The System of the World*. Again he was summoned before the Inquisition at Rome, again was accused of heresy and was compelled by the pope to recant: "I, Galileo, being in my seventieth year, being a prisoner and on my knees, and before your Eminences, having before my eyes the Holy Gospel, which I touch with my hands, abjure, curse and detest the error and the heresy of the movement of the earth."[4]

He had come to Rome on threats from the pope that, if necessary, he would be brought in chains. There he had faced his accusers as a broken old man, exhausted by the intrigues against him and aware of the fate of others who had refused to recant. The next ten years were spent in confinement, apart from family, friends, and his studies. During his confinement he became blind, wasted, and in the end, was denied burial in consecrated ground.

Steps were taken by the Church to eliminate all traces of the Copernican doctrine from the Church colleges and universities throughout Europe. In time, nevertheless, astronomers accepted the double motion of the earth, the rotation on her axis, and the revolution around the sun. But it was 1992, some 349 years after the fact, when the Church admitted that Galileo was correct and an apology of sorts was offered by the pope.

Joseph Campbell once remarked on the contribution made by Galileo in showing that celestial spheres were subject to the same physical laws that apply on earth—and therefore were not the playthings of the gods:

If divinity is to be found anywhere, it will not be "out there," among or beyond the planets. Galileo showed that the same physical laws that govern the movements of bodies on earth apply aloft, to the celestial spheres; and our astronauts, as we have all now seen, have been transported by those earthly laws to the moon. They will soon be on Mars and beyond. Furthermore, we know that the mathematics of those outermost spaces will already have been computed here on earth by human minds. There are no laws out there that are not right here; no gods out there that are not right here, and not only here, but within us, in our minds. So what happens now to those childhood images of the ascent of Elijah, Assumption of the Virgin, Ascension of Christ—all bodily—into heaven?[5]

In regard to the bodily ascension of Christ into heaven, Campbell once noted in a lecture that if Christ had ascended at the speed of light, he would not have cleared our own galaxy by the year 2000—another example that religious beliefs and scientific realities are often difficult to reconcile.

Notes

[1] Andrew Dickson White, *A History of the Warfare of Science with Theology in Christendom*, vol. 1 (New York: D. Appleton-Century, 1936), p. 126.

[2] Ibid., p. 127.

[3] Ibid., p. 138.

[4] Ibid., p. 142.

[5] Joseph Campbell, *Myths to Live By* (New York: Bantam Books, 1973), p. 251.

7

METEOROLOGY: THE BELLS ARE RINGING

As early as the Golden Age of Greece, some philosophers raised the possibility of a natural law that controlled the weather and, particularly, phenomena such as thunder, lightning, hail, and windstorms. Some Roman philosophers were also beginning to look for natural reasons to explain meteorological events. But as the Christian era began, these germs of scientific thought were abandoned as a so-called sacred science spread over the land. Sacred science viewed all meteorological matters as the province of a divine will—the proof of which was found in sacred scripture. And so the Bible came to be the textbook of science.

The interpretation of scriptural passages produced any number of imaginative explanations of the weather. Tertullian (c. 160-230) found passages of scripture proving that lightning was a form of hellfire. Another early father of the Church believed that great arches in the heavens supported a huge cistern filled with water and that angels opened and closed the "windows of heaven"—releasing the water—on command of the Almighty. Albert the Great believed that meteorites were formed from black clouds that contained mud and became stone after being subjected to intense heat. There were even theories taken from the scriptural account of the leviathan, wherein this enormous animal drank from the oceans and then belched, causing the ebb and flow of tides. The basis for these and other theories about the weather came from a belief that religion was the only valid source of knowledge. As noted earlier, St. Augustine (354-430) gave words to this belief in his well-known declaration: "Nothing is to be accepted save on the authority of Scripture, since greater is that authority than all the powers of the human mind."[1]

Throughout the early centuries, there was some consistency of thought with respect to the elements. It was generally believed that the Supreme Being used lightning, wind, and storm to vent his wrath and punish sinners; thus lightning, for example, was the finger of God and rarely struck a man except as punishment for his sins, and the nature of the sins could be inferred from the bodily organs that were hit. When a certain priest was struck by lightning in a sensitive area of the body, therefore, it was evident that he had been punished for the sin of unchastity.

And one may assume that theologians did, on occasion, use the divine wrath as support for their own special interests. We are told, for example, that lightning and hail were held to be punishments for five sins in particular: "impenitence, incredulity, neglect of the repair of churches, fraud in the payment of tithes to the clergy, and oppression of subordinates." As a counter to the possibility of the divine wrath, handbooks for prayer were offered such as the *Spiritual Thunder and Storm Booklet* in 1731, which provided several hundred pages of songs and prayers and outcries such as "sighs for use when it lightens fearfully" and "cries of anguish when the hail storm is drawing on." The booklet was said to handle all meteorological emergencies. At the same time that storms were attributed to the Almighty, however, there occurred a curious contradiction: storms were also attributed to Satan. This belief came about by the early Church recognizing the pagan gods as devils and attributing to their malevolent powers the meteorological ills that affected humankind. As it happened, whether the source of the problem was God or the devil, the same solution to the problem was at hand—the Church, which could both appease the Almighty and offer a defense against the devil.

St. Clement, St. Jerome, St. Augustine, and others found in scripture adequate documentation for a belief that Satan was responsible for bad weather. St. Thomas Aquinas (1225-1274), in his *Summa,* said that "rain and winds, and whatsoever occurs by local impulse alone, can be caused by demons . . . it is a dogma of faith that demons can produce wind storms, and rain of fire from heaven."[2]

And the Catholic theologians were not alone. Protestant authorities such as Martin Luther (1483-1546) and John Wesley (1703-1791) were no less convinced that a diabolical agency was often responsible for storms. Luther, for example, believed that a stone thrown into a certain pond in his native region would cause a storm because the pond was an abode of devils and their prisoners.

Prayer was often used by the faithful to defeat the devil's work, and popes prescribed a number of fetishes and exorcisms to give relief, one of which read, "All the people shall rise, and the priest, turning toward the clouds, shall pronounce the words: 'I exorcise ye, accursed demons, who have dared to use, for the accomplishment of your iniquity, those powers of Nature by which God in divers ways worketh good to mortals; who stir up winds, gather vapors, form clouds and condense them into hail."[3]

Of great repute for many centuries was the pope's own *Agnus Dei,* which was a piece of wax blessed by the pope's own hand and carrying the engraved words "Lamb of God." The manufacture and sale of this fetish was limited to the pope himself, and the ceremony could be performed only on the first and seventh years of his pontificate. It handled everything: hail, pestilence, storms, conflagrations, and enchantments. The prayer that accompanied it was spoken by the pope:

O God ... we humbly beseech thee that thou wilt bless these waxen forms, figured with the image of an innocent lamb ... that, at the touch and sight of them, the faithful may break forth into praises, and that the crash of hailstorms, the blast of hurricanes, the violence of tempests, the fury of winds, and the malice of thunderbolts may be tempered, and evil spirits flee and tremble before the standard of the holy cross, which is graven upon them.[4]

But priests, as well as popes, were thought to have powers over the weather in medieval times. And in the rural sections of France, the peasants were very dependent on their priest. The *Golden Bough* noted that in France, most of the peasants believed that the priest possessed special powers over the elements. Certain prayers, which the priest alone had the right to utter, could change, at least temporarily, the eternal laws of the natural world. The wind, hail, and the rain were thought to be his to command. And fire was also subject to his wishes, and the flames could be extinguished by the priest's spoken word.

The Catholic countries also brought to bear statues and relics of saints who were particularly efficacious in meteorological matters, some excelling in sunshine and others in rain. The Cathedral of Chartres was fortunate to possess relics of St. Taurin, who was especially potent against dry weather, and also some of St. Piat, who was very nearly as infallible against unwanted rain. There were, of course, disappointments along the way and some disillusion with the saints. *The Golden Bough* reports on an episode in Sicily:

By the end of April 1893 there was great distress in Sicily for lack of water. The drought had lasted six months. Every day the sun rose and set in a sky of cloudless blue. The gardens of the Conca d'Oro, which surround Palermo with a magnificent belt of verdure, were withering. Food was becoming scarce. The people were in great alarm. All the most approved methods of procuring rain had been tried without effect. Processions had traversed the streets and the fields. Men, women, and children, telling their beads, had lain whole nights before the holy images. Consecrated candles had burned day and night in the churches. Palm branches, blessed on Palm Sunday, had been spread on the fields. In ordinary years these holy sweepings preserve the crops; but that year, if you will believe me, they had no effect whatever. At Nicosia the inhabitants, bare-headed and barefoot, carried the crucifixes through all the wards of the town and scourged each other with iron whips. It was all in vain. Even the great St. Francis of Paolo himself, who annually performs the miracle of rain and is carried every spring through the market-gardens, either could not or would not help. Masses, vespers, concerts, illuminations, fi re-works—nothing could move him. At last the peasants began to lose patience. Most of the saints were banished. At Palermo they dumped St. Joseph in a garden to see the state of things for himself, and they swore to leave him there in the sun till rain fell. Other saints were turned, like naughty children, with their faces to the wall. Others again, stripped of their beautiful robes, were exiled far from their parishes, threatened, grossly insulted, ducked in horse-ponds. At Caltanisetta the golden wings of St. Michael the Archangel were torn from his shoulders and replaced with wings of pasteboard; his purple mantle taken away and a clout wrapt about him instead. At Licata the patron saint, St. Angelo, fared even worse, for he was left without any garments at all; he was reviled, he was put in irons, he was threatened with drowning or hanging. 'Rain or the rope!' roared the angry people at him, as they shook their fists in his face.[5]

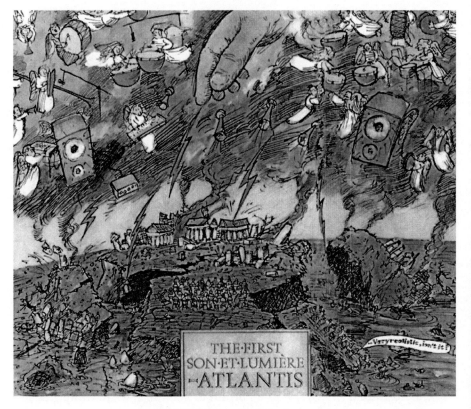

The Hand of God

It was generally believed that God used thunder and lightning to vent
his wrath. The Church suspected the devil might have a hand in it.

(Illustration from *The Way Things Work* by David Macaulay)

Another agent that gave protection against all forms of ill winds
and other troubling events was the church bell. Kings, queens and
popes participated in the baptism of church bells whose peals were
thought to drive away the demons who had inflicted bad weather
on the faithful: "Whensoever this bell shall sound, it shall drive
away the malign influences of the assailing spirits, the horror of

their apparitions, the rush of whirlwinds, the stroke of lightning, the harm of thunder, the disaster of storms, and all the spirits of the tempest."[6]

Unfortunately, however, the evil spirits were not always repulsed by the bells; in fact, it must have seemed as though the grander the cathedral, the more susceptible it was to high-flying spirits and their bolts of lightning. Many of the most prestigious churches were struck repeatedly by lightning and, worse still, often on the bell tower itself. In the eighteenth century, German churches in total had nearly 400 bell towers damaged by lightning in the space of 33 years, and 120 bell ringers were killed.

Of course so long as these evil spirits were invisible, the beliefs about their airborne activities tended to support the authority of the Church and the need for theological assistance; it also served, however, to inhibit the development of any true science or rational explanation of events. Other than this, however, there was little harm done in saying prayers or ringing bells or celebrating the lives of saints who were thought to be instrumental in meteorological matters. But then the forces of Satan took human forms, and there followed a shameful period in history.

Out of old Pagan and Christian beliefs, there evolved the idea that certain men, women, and children had become the agents of Satan and were using wind, hail, flood, and frost for the devil's sinister designs. A belief in witchcraft had taken hold. Superstitions about human beings in cahoots with the devil began in medieval times and, in 1437, was confirmed by Pope Eugene IV, who called for greater diligence against witches who held power over the weather. In 1454, Pope Innocent VIII sent forth his bull *Summis Desiderantes*, which called for the death of sorcerers especially those whose powers over the weather had damaged the vineyards and other crops. In the minds of the faithful, the pope was

Witch-Finder General

Matthew Hopkins was witch-finder general in England and specialized in extracting confessions. Eventually, he was himself condemned for sorcery.

(Mary Evans Picture Library)

Instruments of Torture

Some of the instruments of torture used in the Bamberg witch trials. The Church did not oppose the use of torture or punishment by immolation.

(Mansell Collection/*Time Life*)

exempt from error in such matters and had taken his authority from the scriptural command "Thou shalt not suffer a witch to live,"[7] amongst other scriptural justifications.

A manual was prepared, *Malleus Maleficarum*, which described the means of detecting and punishing witches who caused bad weather. And the records of the Middle Ages hold the confessions of tens of thousands of people, mostly women and children, who were tortured on the rack and later condemned to be burned alive because of superstitions about Satan and a misunderstanding of meteorology.

Some of those accused of witchcraft involving the weather had their legs crushed in boots and others had wedges driven under their fingernails to extort a confession. Matthew Hopkins, a witch finder in England, pierced the bodies of old women with needles to obtain confessions. Hangings and burnings were commonplace, and women accused of witchcraft were often burned in batches. The deathblow to sacred science, at least with respect to meteorology, came in 1752 when Benjamin Franklin brought an electric spark from a cloud—with a kite and a key. In fairly short order, the whole sacred science of meteorology championed by the fathers, the popes, the medieval doctors, and the great theologians, Catholic and Protestant, fell into disrepute. And around Europe and America, on the central spire of many cathedrals, above the relics, altars, and even above the bells, was a lightning rod.

Notes

[1]   Andrew Dickson White, *A History of the Warfare of Science with Theology in Christendom*, vol. 1 (New York: D. Appleton-Century, 1936), p. 325.

[2]   Ibid., p. 337.

[3]   Ibid., p. 341.

[4]   Ibid., p. 343.

[5]   Sir James G. Frazer, *The Golden Bough*, abridged ed. (New York: Macmillan Publishing, 1922), p. 86.

[6]   White, *A History of the Warfare of Science with Theology in Christendom*, p. 346.

[7]   Ibid., p. 352.

8

Geography: The Flat Earth Society

The early religious arguments in support of a flat planet were noted by the historian John William Draper. He quoted Lactantius (c. 240-320) on the heretical notion of a globular earth: "Is it possible that men can be so absurd as to believe that the crops and the trees on the other side of the earth hang downward, and that men have their feet higher than their head?"[1] And St. Augustine (354-430) asserted that "it is impossible there should be inhabitants on the opposite side of the earth, since no such race is recorded by Scripture among the descendants of Adam."[2] Another unanswerable argument against the sphericity of the earth was that in the day of judgment, men on the other side of a globe could not see the Lord descending through the air, a reference to the expected Second Coming of Christ.

There were still other arguments against life on the other side of the earth. One held that Christ would have been obliged to go there and suffer a second time, not to mention the need for a duplicate of the magic garden and Adam and Eve—and no such record of events existed. Another argument noted that the apostles had been charged to go into the world and preach the gospel to all creatures, and there was no record of their having traveled to the opposite side of the earth.

The debate about a globular form of the earth continued into the sixth century when a gentleman named (appropriately enough) Cosmas wrote a work entitled *Christian Topography*, which refuted the heretical idea of a spherical earth and went on to give measurements of the earth's quadrangular plane: four hundred days' journey east and west, half as much north and south. Further, he disclosed that the earth's flat plane was surrounded by mountains on which the sky depended for support.

A globular form also ran counter to another concept of the universe, which showed the universe as a house of sorts, with heaven as its upper story, the earth as its ground floor, and hell as the basement. From this orderly arrangement, religion described the ascension into heaven and descent into the netherworld and the use of winged angels to carry messages between floors. This concept also lent itself to the religious belief that God hung the stars above the world and hurled thunderbolts downward, and on occasion, the floor of heaven was opened by the Almighty to reveal various signs and wonders as well as to dispense rain and snow. White notes, "Nor did this evolution end here. Naturally, in this view of things, if heaven was a loft, hell was a cellar; and if there were ascensions into one, there were descents into the other. Hell being so near, interferences by its occupants with the dwellers of the earth just above were constant, and form a vast chapter in mediaeval literature. Dante made this conception of the location of hell still more vivid, and we find some forms of it serious barriers to geographical investigation. Many a bold navigator, who was quite ready to brave pirates and tempests, trembled at the thought of tumbling with his ship into one of the openings into hell which a widespread belief placed in the Atlantic at some unknown distance from Europe. This terror among sailors was one of the main obstacles in the great voyage of Columbus."[3]

But evidence on the shape of the earth was building in various parts of the world. Muhammadan philosophers and astronomers supported the belief in a globular figure. Sailors noted the circular horizon and became supporters or, at least, curious about the earth's configuration. And at length, the issue was to be settled in a very practical manner when Columbus (1451-1506) set sail without falling off the edge of the world; Vasco da Gama (c. 1469-1529) sailed to India and back, and Magellan (c. 1480-1521) completed a circumnavigation of the globe.

Still, it had taken twelve centuries to gain agreement from the theologians that the earth was indeed round and inhabited on the other side. And some theologians argued the point for another two hundred years after Magellan's voyage until the number of voyages and eyewitness accounts of life on the opposite side (including reports from missionaries) made further argument impossible.

Nevertheless, for some time after the sphericity of the earth was accepted, medieval mapmakers continued some of the old beliefs and showed the habitations of Gog and Magog, the monsters described in the Old Testament. And as the "four winds" were mentioned in the scripture, the mapmaker often showed a depiction of these winds, from which came "a vivid belief in their real existence . . . generally as colossal heads with distended cheeks, blowing vigorously toward Jerusalem." White notes, "After these conceptions had mainly disappeared we find here and there evidences of the difficulty men found in giving up the scriptural idea of direct personal interference by agents of Heaven in the ordinary phenomena of Nature: thus, in a noted map of the sixteenth century representing the earth as a sphere, there is at each pole a crank, with an angel laboriously turning the earth by means of it: and, in another map, the hand of the Almighty, thrust forth from the clouds, holds the earth suspended by a rope and spins it with his thumb and fingers."[5]

Ferdinand Magellan

The circumnavigation of the globe by Magellan disproved the doctrine
of a flat earth. Many assumed his ship was accompanied by gods,
demons, and nymphs.

(The Granger Collection, New York)

There were other examples of geographic truth running afoul of
religion, particularly where scripture seemed to have drawn the map and
suggested the circumstances of life. In the year 1553, a certain Michael
Servetus was on trial for his life and found used against him a quote
he had taken from *Ptolemy's Geography,* in which Judea was described
as mainly a barren, inhospitable area—as opposed to the scriptural
description of "a land flowing with milk and honey." Servetus paid dearly

for his description, which "necessarily inculpated Moses, and grievously outraged the Holy Ghost."[6] His antagonist at the trial was John Calvin.

The Bible was also used to establish the amount of the earth's surface that was covered with water. Two verses in scripture (Esdras 2:42, 47) spoke to this question:

> Upon the third day thou didst command that the waters should be gathered in the seventh part of the earth; six parts hast thou dried up and kept them to the intent that of these some, being planted of God and tilled, might serve thee.

> Upon the fifth day thou saidst unto the seventh part where the waters were gathered, that it should bring forth living creatures, fowls and fishes and so it came to pass.

There was no doubting the authority of these statements, and the fathers of the Church subscribed to them totally. On the positive side, the belief that only one-seventh of the earth's surface was covered with water led many to believe that the oceans were narrower than supposed, thereby encouraging navigators such as Columbus. And many sailors of the time needed encouragement, given the widespread belief that the Atlantic Ocean had holes that opened into hell.

Another misconception in the geography of the world was that its center was located in the holy, or capital, city of the culture in question. Thus did the Egyptians believe that Thebes was the center of the world, and the Jews, Jerusalem. Likewise, the Assyrians believed the world centered on Babylon; the Hindus, on Mount Meru; the Muhammadans, on Mecca; and the Greeks, on Olympus or the Temple at Delphi.

There was ample evidence to support claims of centricity. Jerusalem, for example, was described as the center of the earth in the book of Ezekiel. This was confirmed on the authority of St. Jerome, the preeminent biblical scholar of the early Church and reiterated by churchmen over many centuries, including Pope Urban. Dante glorified Jerusalem as the center of the world, and a noted traveler in the Middle Ages confirmed in writing that a spear standing erect at the Holy Sepulchre in Jerusalem would cast no shadow at the equinox. In time, it was concluded by the Christian thinkers that the geographical center of the world was in Jerusalem, at the Church of the Holy Sepulchre, and that here marked the site of the cross of Christ and the magic tree that bore the forbidden fruit. The medieval mapmakers, therefore, were so guided in their efforts to accurately diagram the world.

One of the more telling comments about the concept of a flat earth came from the missionary Acosta—who found himself on the other side of the world but still landed on his feet, so to speak. Acosta wrote home, "Whatsoever Lactantius saieth, wee that live now at Peru, and inhabite that parte of the worlde which is opposite to Asia and their Antipodes, finde not ourselves to bee hanging in the aire, our heades downward and our feete on high."[7]

Notes

1   John William Draper, *History of the Conflict between Religion and Science* (New York: D. Appleton, 1922), p. 64.

2   Ibid., p. 64.

3   Andrew Dickson White, *A History of the Warfare of Science with Theology in Christendom*, vol. 1 (New York: D. Appleton-Century, 1936), p. 96.

4   Draper, *History of the Conflict between Religion and Science*, p. 161.

5   White, *A History of the Warfare of Science with Theology in Christendom*, p. 101.

6   Ibid., p. 113.

7   Ibid., p. 110.

9

ARCHEOLOGY: THE ANTIQUITY OF HUMANS

In the second century, Theophilus, the bishop of Antioch, concluded that the world began six thousand years before Christ based on a projection of the six days of Creation and the scriptural reference: "One day is with the Lord as a thousand years."[1] The certainty of the date was made abundantly clear by St. Augustine and others who regarded any substantial deviation from this date as a deadly heresy.

Over the centuries, theologians confirmed and reconfirmed a series of dates, but none going beyond 6,000 BCE when, as Luther pointed out, "We know, on the authority of Moses that longer ago than six thousand years the world did not exist."[2]

Then in 1650, an authoritative calculation came from Archbishop Ussher (1581-1656), a very influential theologist in Christendom. In his book *Annals of the Ancient and New Testaments*, he set the date of creation at 4004 BCE, and his estimate was taken as the final word. Even Christian theologians who quarreled on other issues accepted Ussher's date for the antiquity of humans—until an even more definitive calculation came from a Dr. John Lightfoot (1828-1889), vice chancellor of the University of Cambridge, who concluded that "heaven and earth, center and circumference, were created together, in the same instant, and clouds full of water . . . this work took place and man was created by the Trinity on the twenty-third of October, 4004 B.C.E., at nine o'clock in the morning."[3] This led Bertrand Russell (1872-1970), the philosopher, to waggishly observe that "one might believe, without risk of heresy, that Adam and Eve came into existence on October 16 or October 30 provided that your reasons were derived from Genesis."[4]

Around 1850, however, some disquieting findings came from a number of Egyptologists who found evidence of an Egyptian civilization that preceded the accepted date of Creation (4004 BCE) by quite some time. In fact, evidence came to show that Egyptian civilization was in a very advanced state on the date of Creation, and artifacts found in deposits along the Nile and dated according to the rate of earthy deposits placed Egyptian civilization thousands on thousands of years before the date given by the sacred chronologists.

Another disquieting fact emerged concerning the sacred date given for Noah's flood. It appeared that in the long records of Egyptian civilization, there was no mention of a flood or any indication that, on the presumed date of the flood, anything had happened to interrupt the smooth course of Egyptian history. The written records seemed to be confirmed also by very ancient sun-dried brick that predated the sacred deluge and yet remained untouched by any watery evidence.

It would be difficult to overestimate the findings of the Egyptologists on our own understanding of the origins of the Jewish and Christian faiths. White's book included this description:

> Egyptologists have also translated for us the old Nile story of *The Two Brothers*, and have shown, as we have already seen, that one of the most striking parts of our sacred Joseph legend was drawn from it; they have been obliged to admit that the story of the exposure of Moses in the basket of rushes, his rescue, and his subsequent greatness, had been previously told, long before

Moses's time, not only of King Sargon, but of various other great personages of the ancient world; they have published plans of Egyptian temples and copies of the sculptures upon their walls, revealing the earlier origin of some of the most striking features of the worship and ceremonial claimed to have been revealed especially to the Hebrews; they have found in the *Egyptian Book of the Dead,* and in various inscriptions of the Nile temples and tombs, earlier sources of much in the ethics so long claimed to have been revealed only to the chosen people in the Book of the Covenant, in the ten commandments, and elsewhere; they have given to the world copies of the Egyptian texts showing that the theology of the Nile was one of various fruitful sources of later ideas, statements, and practices regarding the brazen serpent, the golden calf, trinities, miraculous conceptions, incarnations, resurrections, ascensions, and the like, and that Egyptian sacro-scientific ideas contributed to early Jewish and Christian sacred literature statements, beliefs, and even phrases regarding the Creation, astronomy, geography, magic, medicine, diabolical influences, with a multitude of other ideas, which we also find coming into early Judaism in greater or less degree from Chaldean and Persian sources.[5]

From very early times, archeologists had been coming up with more evidence relating to the antiquity of humankind. People in various parts of the world had been finding rude stone weapons, some crudely chipped and some with greater polish, but all of a kind that could not be related to the current civilization. So they assumed that these implements must have been weapons of the gods—the larger ones thunderbolts and the smaller ones arrowheads—and gave them the apt name thunderstones. It was assumed that thunderstones had been hurled around heaven by supernatural personages and fallen to earth in the process; due to their sacred nature, then, they were often used in the walls and altars of temples. Later, the stones came to be venerated in their own right as weapons used during the "war in heaven" to abolish Satan and his demons. In the twelfth century, the bishop of Rennes asserted the value of thunderstones as "a divinely appointed means of securing success in battle, safety on the sea, security against thunder, and immunity from unpleasant dreams."[6]

Gradually, more thunderstones and other relics of earlier civilizations were uncovered, and despite the efforts of the clergy, it appeared that such stone implements must be associated with an earlier period in human history—a far earlier period than anything even hinted at in sacred scriptures.

And then came the bones. Along with stone implements came the remains of human bones buried with the remains of animals that were long extinct. By the beginning of the nineteenth century, chipped flint implements and human skulls and bones appeared in a continuing series of geologic discoveries, and although geology was still denounced as a black art by many of the clergy, the balance of thought had begun to shift.

Today, if we were to date the creation of human beings, we would first be obliged to define which point on the continuum of evolution that we recognized as "humankind." Archeologists have shown that agriculture and civilization began at about 12,000 BCE. But before that, human beings with an intelligence equal to ours today existed as gatherers and hunters. *Cro-Magnon* man (30,000 BCE) was indistinguishable from contemporary man, and *Neanderthal* man (150,000 BCE) had a brain somewhat larger than our own. *Neanderthal* man also stood and walked upright, and although he had a heavier browridge and receding chin and forehead, Neanderthal man was essentially the same as modern man. Farther back in time was *Homo erectus* (1.5 million years ago) who still more closely resembled a human being than an ape, a characteristic

BEGINNING OF THE UNIVERSE

	Approximate Beginning*	An Example of Creation
Man/Ape	4 MYA	Java Man
Mammals	60 MYA	Lemurs
Reptiles	225 MYA	Crocodilia
Amphibia	550 MYA	Dawn Tadpole
Ocean Life	4,500 MYA	Jellyfish
Solar System	5,000 MYA	Solar System
Galaxies Expanding	10,000 MYA	Galaxies Expanding
Big Bang Theory	15,000 MYA	Big Bang

** MYA = Millions of years ago.

(Adapted from *Beginnings*, by Isaac Asimov)

This Old World

Although the Church taught that everything in the universe was created instantaneously in 4004 BCE, science now estimates the universe began billions of years ago and developed in stages.

now described as a hominin. Australopithecus (4.0 million years ago) was neither human nor ape but was closer to human beings based on an ability to walk upright. Over the last hundred years, paleoanthropologists have recovered from the earth an almost continuous evolutionary record of forms, including monkeys, apes, and humankind, leaving no doubts concerning the origins and evolution of the human species.[7]

Evolution continues backward through the age of mammals, of reptiles, of amphibia, and other forms of life to a prelife period about 15,000 million years ago when our universe was created. Bishop Ussher would have been surprised. Dr. Lightfoot might have asked whether it was AM or PM.

Notes

[1]   Andrew Dickson White, *A History of the Warfare of Science with Theology in Christendom*, vol. 1 (New York: D. Appleton-Century, 1936), p. 250.

[2]   Ibid., p. 252.

[3]   White, *A History of the Warfare of Science with Theology in Christendom*, vol. 1, p. 9.

[4]   Bertrand Russell, *Religion and Science* (New York: Oxford University Press, 1961), p. 52.

[5]   White, *A History of the Warfare of Science with Theology in Christendom*, vol. 2, p. 375.

[6]   White, *A History of the Warfare of Science with Theology in Christendom*, vol. 1, p. 266.

[7]   Richard E. Leakey and Roger Lewin, *Origins* (New York: Dutton, 1977), p. 352.

10

GEOLOGY: OF GIANTS AMONG MEN

In the seventeenth and eighteenth centuries, more attention was being given to human origins and those of other life-forms. But the sacred science of the time stumbled rather badly with respect to fossil remains and where they fit in to the master plan of Creation. The Church again looked for answers in holy writ and, again, was led to some curious conclusions.

As background, early theologians such as St. Augustine (354-430) and the Venerable Bede (673-735), followed by eighteenth-century theologians, supported the idea that death itself entered the world because of the transgression of Adam and Eve, as did earthquakes, volcanoes, fires, and other unpleasant phenomena of nature. And then geology came along with the suggestion that earthquakes, volcanoes, and even death (of animals) had been occurring long before man or woman put in an appearance on the planet.

Such findings indicated that the creation of the universe was older than the Church supposed and that the creation was not an instantaneous act, but a series of events that occurred in an unknown sequence. As a result, geology was thought to be a dangerous study leading to infidelity and atheism and apt to depose the Creator from his throne. The poet Cowper addressed the issue in these words:

> Some drill and bore The solid earth, and from the stata there Extract a register, by which we learn That He who made it, and revealed its date to Moses, was mistaken in its age!

An early and important proof of the age of the world and the evolution of life is the record of fossils, and as noted, attempts to explain fossil remains stirred a number of lively debates and imaginative solutions. In his book *Beginnings*, Isaac Asimov notes some early attempts at an explanation: "Such fossils were noted even in ancient times, but most people didn't know what to make of them. There were suggestions that they were just freaks of nature or that they were part of a life force that made even rocks strive to bring forth something with the appearance of life. During the Middle Ages, there were suggestions that fossils were Satan's attempt to imitate the work of God in creating life, and of course Satan failed miserably. Others held that perhaps God had tried making life until he was sure he had it right and that fossils were his practice shots, so to speak."[1]

A similar theory was published as recently as 1853, under the title of *A Brief and Complete Refutation of the Anti-scriptural Theory of Geologists*, wherein it was supposed that fossil remains were "the organisms found in the depths of the earth made on the first of the six creative days, as models for the plants and animals to be created on the third, fifth and sixth days."[2]

In another initiative, theologians attempted to persuade the faithful that fossils did not precede Creation, but came at the same time and had only been made to look more ancient for purposes of authenticity—the seashore, then, was covered with shells that had never been inhabited, but only gave the appearance of a prior existence. Chateaubriand, in his *Genius of Christianity* noted, "It was part of the perfection and harmony of the nature which was displayed before men's eyes that the deserted nests of last year's birds should be seen on the trees, and that the seashore should be covered with shells which had been the abode of fish, and yet the world was quite new, and nests and shells had never been inhabited."[3]

Along the same lines, in 1857, the English naturalist Philip Henry Gosse, in his book *Omphalos*, attempted to save the literal interpretation of Genesis by declaring that changes in the earth's surface—in rocks, minerals, and fossils—were simply "appearances" and were in fact created at the same time and in the same instant as humans and animals. And included in his considerations were the fossilized footprints of birds, reptiles, and the skeletons of mammoths. The difficulty in Gosse's theory of instantaneous creation was evident to some in that fossil remains included "the half digested remains of weaker animals found in the fossilized bodies of the stronger, the marks of hyenas' teeth on fossilized bones found in various caves, and even the skeleton of the Siberian mammoth at St. Petersburg with lumps of flesh bearing the marks of wolves teeth."[4] And it seemed unlikely that the prey would have been created only to be consumed instantaneously by the predator. The preface to Gosse's book hoped that the work would reconcile the views of science on religion, but at the close of his book, he repeated the irrefutable testimony from scripture that, in six days, Jehovah created heaven and earth, the seas, and everything in them.

When it appeared that fossils were here to stay, theologians took the position that the reality of fossils did not precede, but rather followed, the year 4004 BCE, which Ussher (1581-1656) had calculated to be the beginning of the world; in this case, fossils could be life-forms that had died and been deposited at the time of Noah's flood. This became the accepted theory in Christendom for several centuries and overcame any objection that God had been imperfect in creating life forms that, by some caprice, had become extinct.

Along the way, there were a number of interesting interpretations of fossil findings. St. Augustine thought that a fossil tooth, which had been found in North Africa, must have come from one of the giants mentioned in scripture. The French Benedictine Calmet, in the eighteenth century, believed that the mastodon's bones were those of an ancient king—one of the giants—who had been a victim of the deluge. Similar reports of "the bones of giants" came from Spain, England, and America, and the bones of mammoths were displayed in public places as "giants mentioned in Scripture." This provoked a certain Henrion to draw up tables that showed the size of our antediluvian ancestors; the height of Adam was 123 feet 9 inches, and Eve was 118 feet 9 inches. So for a time, theologians took comfort in the idea that Noah's flood explained the presence of fossils and, moreover, that discoveries of large fossil bones confirmed the scriptural accounts of giants in the ancient world.

One of the first persons to close in on the true nature of fossils was Leonardo da Vinci in the sixteenth century, and his ideas were picked up and expanded on in other parts of Europe. But it was still several centuries before the Church relinquished its centuries-old belief that fossil remains were the result of the deluge.

In part, the examination of the Assyrian tablets in the British museum in 1872 clinched the case for geology. It was found that the accounts of Creation in Genesis were based largely on adaptations of earlier Chaldean myths and legends and, particularly, the account of the deluge. As a result, Christian scholars could no longer easily accept the authenticity of the deluge described in Genesis or use it as the basis for explaining fossils.

Giants among Men

Greek mythology produced a number of impressive giants, some with a taste for humans. Following on, the Bible also credited the existence of giants in earlier times.

(Arvis Stewart)

The discoveries coming from the Assyrian tablets came too late for Voltaire. He was opposed to the sacred books of the Jews but, at the same time, had to explain the discovery of marine fossils in various elevated areas of Europe. Apparently, he rose to the occasion by supposing that the remains of fossil fishes were spoilage that had simply been discarded by travelers and, likewise, that marine fossil shells had simply been discarded by tourists on their return home from the shore.

Seismology and theology were also at odds. Theologians, unable to explain earthquakes in any other way, interpreted them as signs that humanity had angered the Almighty, beginning with the transgressions of Adam and Eve. All the great theologians lined up behind this theory, which prevailed for close to two thousand years. The Protestant leader John Wesley (1703-1791) gave a sermon on "The Cause and Cure of Earthquakes"[5] in which he said that those who believe in scripture must believe that sin is the moral cause of earthquakes, regardless of what their natural cause may be, and went on to relate earthquakes to the sins of Adam and Eve so that earthquakes were God's works of judgment, the deserved punishment of sin.

One of the champions of geologic science was Sir Charles Lyell (1797-1875), a British geologist, who would have been gratified to hear the sermon given at his funeral:

> The late Dean of Westminster, Dr. Arthur Stanley, was widely known and beloved on both continents. In his memorial sermon after the funeral of Sir Charles Lyell he said: "It is now clear to diligent students of the Bible that the first and second chapters of Genesis contain two narratives of the creation side by side, differing from each other in almost every particular of time and place and order. It is well known that, when the science of geology first arose, it was involved in endless schemes of attempted reconciliation with the letter of Scripture."[6]

So there were various attempts to reconcile geologic findings with the letter of scripture, but perhaps none could surpass the representation of mammoth bones as the giants mentioned in scripture—and Henrion's studied estimate that Adam and Eve had measured some 120 feet in height. His eighteenth-century audience must have felt very small, indeed.

As archeology and geology had combined to challenge the Church's surmise about the date of Creation, both of the earth and its inhabitants, anthropology added to the evidence and also challenged the idea that the human race had taken a Fall. And it was no small issue to theologians because the premise of a Fall was necessary to explain the presence of evil and imperfection in a world that was the personal handiwork of the Creator.

Notes

1 Isaac Asimov, *Beginnings* (New York: Berkley Books, 1989), p. 48.

2 Andrew Dickson White, *A History of the Warfare of Science with Theology in Christendom*, vol. 1 (New York: D. Appleton-Century, 1936), p. 240.

3 Ibid., p. 231.

4 Ibid., p. 240.

5 Ibid., p. 220.

6 Ibid., p. 247.

11

ANTHROPOLOGY: THE FALL OF HUMANKIND

From early times, there have been different views of our human development. One view was that human beings were created perfect in every respect—physically, intellectually, and morally—when they first appeared on earth. There was no sin or pain or disappointment because the Creator had fashioned humans to perfection. There was even no death, for humans (and animals) were created to live forever by the grace and power of a supreme being.

Perhaps the idea of human perfection began as an acknowledgment that a supreme being should be capable of perfection in his creations, that they should, in every way, reflect the glory of his being. The problem, obviously, was that perfection hardly represented the real circumstances of life on this planet. And so humankind had to take a Fall in order to explain its present predicament. And as the Fall was the fault of humans, it preserved the image of a capable and caring Creator.

Those who study ancient myths record many stories of a Fall long before the Old Testament and the biblical account of Adam and Eve. Joseph Campbell (1904-1987) in his book *Myths to Live By* finds "the symbolism of the serpent, tree and garden of immortality already in the earliest cuneiform texts, depicted on Old Sumerian cylinder seals and represented even in the arts and rites of primitive village folk throughout the world." The story of the Fall in the Bible, Campbell notes, is instructional on the level of "a nursery tale of disobedience and its punishment, inculcating an attitude of dependency, fear and respectful devotion, such as might be appropriate for a child in relation to a parent."[1]

The prophet Zoroaster preached a Fall in the ancient Persian religion, wherein the god Ahura Mazda created a perfect world entirely free of pain and despair, but his perfect creation was then marred by an opposing evil spirit, Angra Minyu, who brought about a Fall and introduced evil and ignorance into the world. Although the powers of darkness were not caused directly by the human race, people were obliged to choose between good and evil—and many fell on the wrong side. Zoroastrianism was still able to offer, like Christianity, hope for a better tomorrow through the intercession of a savior, Saoshyant, who promised the resurrection of the body after death and thereafter a purified soul, both of which would enjoy an eternal life.

Greek mythology also had its legend of a Fall, wherein Hesiod (eighth century BCE) reported a revelation that men in the most ancient times were "a golden race"—who lived like gods without cares, labor, or illnesses—and were surrounded by fruitful fields and flocks; and when they died, it was as if they were only overcome by sleep. But then came the well-known Pandora, who opened a vase bidden by divine command to remain closed, and let loose a torrent of troubles, sorrows, and disease in the world. The problems in the world, then, have long been associated with a failure not of the gods but of humans such as Pandora and, of course, Eve.

The Jewish and Christian story of the Fall was no less wondrous than the earlier Greek or Persian myths—which undoubtedly influenced the biblical account. Joseph Campbell condenses the story in his *Myths to Live By*:

In relation to the first books and chapters of the Bible, it used to be the custom of both Jews and Christians to take the narratives literally, as though they were dependable accounts of the origin of the universe and of actual prehistoric events. It was supposed and taught that there had been, quite concretely, a creation of the world in seven days by a god known only to the Jews; that somewhere on this broad new earth there had been a Garden of Eden containing a serpent that could talk; that the first woman, Eve, was formed from the first man's rib, and that the wicked serpent told her of the marvelous properties of the fruits of a certain tree of which God had forbidden the couple to eat; and that, as a consequence of their having eaten of that fruit, there followed a 'Fall' of all mankind, death came into the world, and the couple was driven forth from the garden. For there was in the center of that garden a second tree, the fruit of which would have given them eternal life; and their creator, fearing lest they should now take and eat of that too, and so become as knowing and immortal as himself, cursed them, and having driven them out, placed at his garden gate 'cherubim and a flaming sword which turned every way to guard the way to the tree of life.' It seems impossible today, but people actually believed all that until as recently as half a century or so ago.[2]

So once again, theologians took the story of Genesis quite literally. Even at the time of the Reformation, Martin Luther (1483-1546) commented on Adam and Eve in terms of the following: "They entered into the garden about noon, and having a desire to eat, she took the apple; then came the fall—according to our account at about two o'clock."[3]

Similarly, literal interpretations of sacred text were made by theologians such as John Wesley (1703-1791), who believed that "death entered the world by sin."[4] This implied that death was unknown before the Fall. It was just such a literal belief in the story of Genesis that confounded the attempts of scientists to put forward other hypotheses concerning the development of mankind. In the case of the Fall, for example, the Church was bound to deny any findings that suggested the universe was created before the date given the Garden of Eden and evolution of any sort was, by definition, unacceptable in a scheme wherein humans and animals were created to perfection at the outset. Evolution implied the rise or upward tendency of humankind while the Fall implied the reverse.

Many advances in knowledge had contributed to the idea that the Fall was not supportable, but a special contribution was made by the scholars who found in the Ninevite records "the undoubted source of that form of the fall legend which was adopted by the Hebrews and by them transmitted to Christianity."[5] The story of Genesis, then, had not come directly from the Creator but rather from myths and legends that predated the biblical account. And myths of a Fall were found to be prevalent in many ages and cultures, all serving to explain the existence of evil and the hardships of life and perhaps adding a measure of dependency and discipline to the lives of the faithful.

Now, in the first century before Christ, there had been some Greek philosophers, also several Roman poets and philosophers, who developed prophetic insights into a so-called upward tendency of humankind. Lucretius (c. 96-55 BCE) described the rude beginnings of civilization and Horace (65-8 BCE) pictured early man as a cave dweller with primitive stone weapons who, over time, advanced through inventions, literature, and law. Thoughts of this kind, however, were apparently overwhelmed by the Jewish and then Christian beliefs in the Fall.

The Fall of Animals and Plants

Just as humans needed an explanation of why they, made in the image of God, were nevertheless imperfect, so did they need an explanation of why all of God's creatures were flawed, and so the animal kingdom came under question, particularly those animals that appeared to be superfluous or even noxious. Why would a benevolent God create lions and snakes and other species that threatened men and women? Or insects that had little function other than to annoy humans and perhaps damage crops? The answer was clear: the disobedience of Adam and Eve had led the Almighty to punish the world. Sin was the cause of good animals being turned into bad; before the Fall, there was neither fang nor claw nor venom to trouble the world. Over the centuries, this conclusion was reached and repeated by the great minds of the Church.

- St. Augustine (354-430) affirmed that the animal kingdom (and vegetable) was cursed as a result of the Fall.

- Two hundred years later, St. Bede said, "Thus fierce and poisonous animals were created for terrifying man [because God foresaw that he would sin], in order that he might be made aware of the final punishment of Hell."[6]

- The twelfth century saw Peter Lombard's great theological work, *Sentences*, state, "No created things would have been hurtful to man had he not sinned; they became hurtful for the sake of terrifying and punishing vice or proving and perfecting virtue; they were created harmless, and on account of sin became hurtful."[7]

- And still in the eighteenth century, John Wesley declared with certainty that before the Fall "none of these attempted to devour or in any wise hurt one another; the spider was as harmless as the fly and did not lie in wait for blood."[8]

THE FALL OF MAN.

Man was by Heaven made to govern all,
But how unfit, demonstrates in his fall,
Created pure, and with strength endu'd
Of grace divine, sufficient to have stood,
But alienate from God he soon became
The child of wrath, pride, misery and shame.

The Fall of Man

A mythical Adam and Eve explains the existence of evil in a world supposedly created by an all-powerful and all-loving God. Many societies had Fall myths.

(Folk Art Museum, MSU)

If after the Fall, innocent animals had become ferocious in order to terrify humans, the intent to terrify was furthered by the creation of imaginative new and even more frightening species. White notes this pious spirit influenced scientific thought and pervaded the art of the Middle Ages, particularly in the cathedrals:

> In the gargoyles overhanging the walls, in the grotesques clambering about the towers or perched upon pinnacles, in the dragons prowling under archways or lurking in bosses of foliage, in the apocalyptic beasts carved upon the stalls of the choir, stained into the windows, wrought into the tapestries, illuminated in the letters and borders of psalters and missals, these marvels of creation suggested everywhere morals from the Physiologus, the Bestiaries, and the Exempla.[9]

Another example of the terrifying aspect of animals was typified in *The Properties of Things*, a work by the English Franciscan Bartholomew:

> Naturally this good Franciscan naturalist devotes much thought to the "dragons" mentioned in Scripture. He says: "The dragon is most greatest of all serpents, and oft he is drawn out of his den and riseth up into the air, and the air is moved by him, and also the sea swelleth against his venom, and he hath a crest, and reareth his tongue, and hath teeth like a saw, and hath strength, and not only in teeth but in tail, and grieveth with biting and with stinging. Whom he findeth he slayeth. Oft four or five of them fasten their tails together and rear up their heads, and sail over the sea to get good meat. Between elephants and dragons is everlasting fighting; for the dragon with his tail spanneth the elephant, and the elephant with his nose throweth down the dragon.... The cause why the dragon desireth his blood is the coldness therof, by the which the dragon desireth to

cool himself. Jerome saith that the dragon is a full thirsty beast, insomuch that he openeth his mouth against the wind to quench the burning of his thirst in that wise. Therefore, when he seeth ships in great wind he flieth against the sail to take the cold wind, and overthroweth the ship."[10]

One of the most maligned creatures was the serpent on account of its direct involvement with Adam and Eve. It was believed that the Almighty had punished the serpent for its trespasses, but that before that sinful episode all serpents stood erect, walked, and of course, talked. In the eighteenth century, one of the more prominent and prolific of the theologic writers, Watson, concluded there was no reason to believe that the serpent had a serpentine form until its transformation; at that point, it was degraded to a reptile and made to travel on its belly as a means of punishment and humiliation.

Many forms of life were not dangerous but were at least irritating or unnecessary, and this also gave rise to speculation on why the Almighty should have created them. Some of the greatest minds were stumped, according to White:

Troublesome questions also arose among theologians regarding animals classed as "superfluous." St. Augustine was especially exercised thereby. He says: "I confess I am ignorant why mice and frogs were created, or flies and worms . . . . All creatures are either useful, hurtful, or superfluous to us . . . . As for the hurtful creatures, we are either punished, or disciplined, or terrified by them, so that we may not cherish and live this life." As to the "superfluous animals," he says, "Although they are not necessary for our service, yet the whole design of the universe is thereby completed and finished." Luther, who followed St. Augustine in so many other matters, declined to follow him fully in this. To him a fly was not merely superfluous, it was noxious—sent by the devil to vex him when reading.[11]

In time, some naturalists and theologians attempted to justify the superfluous and noxious animals by attributing positive qualities to them. John Ray of England's Royal Society was one who argued, in the seventeenth century, that there was a divine purpose to all life and that the goodness and wisdom of the Almighty was apparent in that "if nettles sting, it is to secure an excellent medicine for children and cattle . . . if the bramble hurts man, it makes all the better hedge for if it chances to prick the owner, it tears the thief . . . weasels, kites and other hurtful animals induce us to watchfulness; thistles and moles to good husbandry; lice oblige us to cleanliness in our bodies, spiders in our houses, and the moth in our clothes."[12]

However weak the reasoning, the effect of Ray's thinking was to suggest that sin was not responsible for all the evil in the animal and plant kingdoms. Still, some philosophers poked fun at the idea of such a carefully planned creation—Goethe made sport of it in a verse that praised the forethought of the Creator in planning for the cork tree, which ultimately would furnish stoppers for wine bottles.

The Fall, then, was an explanation of every imperfection and problem that humans encountered. The Fall caused furrows and craters in the earth's surface, which had formerly been as smooth as an egg; evil in men and women who otherwise were created in the image of God; ferocity in some animals and irritating qualities in others; and hurtful prickers on plants, which had theretofore been harmless. Were it not for the Fall, men and women, in their innocence, would have lived forever in a literal heaven on earth.

Notes

1   Joseph Campbell, *Myths to Live By* (New York: Bantam Books, 1973), p. 29.

2   Ibid., p. 23.

3   Andrew Dickson White, *A History of the Warfare of Science with Theology in Christendom*, vol. 1 (New York: D. Appleton—Century, 1936), p. 288.

4   Ibid., p. 289.

5   Ibid., p. 301.

6   Ibid., p. 28.

7   Ibid., p. 29.

8   Ibid., p. 29.

9   Ibid., p. 36.

10   Ibid., p. 34.

11   Ibid., p. 30.

12

BIOLOGY: ON THE SIDE OF ANGELS

Well before the sacred books of the Hebrews, the Chaldeo-Babylonian and Egyptian civilizations conceived of a creation that was both instantaneous and complete. And it is now realized that the substance of these early concepts found their way into the sacred books of the Hebrews and, from there, into the Christian concepts of Creation. In this scenario, humans and animals alike were created at a single point—all species were represented from the outset, and none were subject to modification (or extinction) ever afterward.

But of equally ancient origin was another concept of creation that believed, in effect, that some living things were the result of continuous growth, or an evolution. In ancient Egypt, some thinkers believed that the sun-god created animals and humans out of lifeless slime and, also, that insects and some of the lesser animals might have been produced at a later date, from secondary sources such as decayed matter. A number of ancient Greeks picked up on this idea, and Aristotle, in particular, spoke of "a perfecting principle" in nature that gave rise to a rudimentary theory of evolution.

Even a number of theologians, including St. Gregory and St. Augustine (354-430), gave voice to the idea that certain minor forms of life may have come about through a growth process, or second stage of creation. St. Augustine noted that some very small animals and insects may not have been created on the fifth and sixth days, but may have originated later, possibly from putrefying matter. God, of course, was held to be the author of these secondary causes wherein bees were generated from decomposed veal, beetles came from horseflesh, and grasshoppers from mules. In support of this doctrine of secondary creation, St. Augustine noted the biblical account of Nebuchadnezzar, wherein "human beings had been changed into animals, especially into swine, wolves, and owls."[1] The same essential idea of second causes was also taken up by St. Thomas Aquinas (1225-1274).

Some of the impetus for a consideration of second causes may have come from a growing concern over reconciling the sacred narratives with the vast assemblage of creatures, great and small, that came to be observed. Of course, miracles could explain a great deal, but a second-causes concept lessened the need to depend on the miraculous and tended to preserve the literalism of the biblical account:

> This idea of a development by secondary causes apart from the original creation was helped in its growth by a theological exigency. More and more, as the organic world was observed, the vast multitude of petty animals, winged creatures, and "creeping things" was felt to be a strain upon the sacred narrative. More and more it became difficult to reconcile the dignity of the Almighty with his work in bringing each of these creatures before Adam to be named; or to reconcile the human limitations of Adam with his work in naming "every living creature"; or to reconcile the dimensions of Noah's ark with the space required for preserving all of them, and the food of all sorts necessary for their sustenance, whether they were admitted by twos, as stated in one scriptural account, or by sevens, as stated in the other.[2]

In spite of the concept of second causes, however, the main body of theological thought continued to be that "every species in the animal kingdom now exists as it left the hands of the Creator, the naming process by Adam, and the door of Noah's ark."[3] And the Church was to close the door on thoughts of evolution for over a thousand years.

By the seventeenth century some of the more thoughtful theologians once again began to grapple with the problems associated with a belief in the Genesis version of animal creation. It was becoming more and more apparent that the world contained a far greater number of species than had once been imagined—so numerous that it began to seem unlikely that the Almighty had created and then given names to hordes of insects and animals, and equally unlikely that they could have been gathered by Noah and accommodated on the ark. The ark therefore tended to become larger in written accounts, and the years given to its construction longer.

A particular problem arose in trying to explain the distribution of animal life around the world. Since after the flood, all animals were located on top of Mt. Ararat; they had to find their way over great distances, high mountains, and even great oceans. So theologians pondered how so sluggish an animal as the sloth had found its way to South America. The kangaroo could not have reached Australia unless a causeway of sorts spanned the ocean, and if it did, why had not lions, tigers, and bears also traveled to this far-off continent? Some believed that men must have transported animals across the ocean in boats, but on reflection, it seemed unlikely that certain dangerous, unclean, or otherwise objectionable species would have been sought as traveling companions. The agency of angels had also been used to explain the distribution of animals to remote areas, but "finally it overtaxed even the theological imagination to conceive of angels, in obedience to the divine command, distributing the various animals over the earth, dropping the megatherium in South America, the archeopteryx in Europe, the ornithorhynchus in Australia, and the opossum in North America."[4]

But then the proofs of a growth process began to emerge, and philosophers, astronomers, and naturalists began to discuss the possibility of an evolutionary process. One of the first to speculate on an evolutionary process of sorts was Giordano Bruno (1548-1600) who, for his impious thoughts, was burned at the stake. In the seventeenth and eighteenth centuries, a number of scientists prompted concepts of evolution in the solar system, in planets, and in animal life. Descartes (1596-1650) led the way in astronomy, but his theories were resisted and repressed by theologians. De Maillet (1656-1738) began speculation on the origin of animal forms and the transformation of species—a great deal of his profound thought, however, was made vulnerable by his proposal that the first human being was born of a mermaid.

Linnaeus (1707-1778) shocked the ecclesiastical authorities with proofs of a sexual system in plants. Buffon (1707-1788) was obliged by the authorities to recant his theories relating to the evolution of animal life. Treviranus (1776-1837) and Lamarck (1744-1829) contributed important, if sometimes mistaken, ideas to the concept of evolution, as did Geoffrey Saint-Hilaire (1772-1844). From Treviranus came, in 1802, his work on biology, and in this he gave forth the idea that from forms of life originally simple had arisen all higher organizations by gradual development, that every living creature had a capacity for receiving modifications of its structure from external influences, and that no species had become really extinct, but that each had passed into some other species. From Lamarck came about the same time his researches, and a little later, his *Zoölogical Philosophy*, which introduced a new factor into the process of evolution—the action of the animal itself in its efforts toward a development to suit new needs—and he gave as his principal conclusions the following:

1. Life tends to increase the volume of each living body and of all its parts up to a limit determined by its own necessities.

2. New wants in animals give rise to new organs.

3. The development of these organs is in proportion to their employment.

4. New developments may be transmitted to offspring.

His well-known examples to illustrate these views, such as that of successive generations of giraffes lengthening their necks by stretching them to gather high-growing foliage and of successive generations of kangaroos lengthening and strengthening their hind legs by the necessity of keeping themselves erect while jumping, provoked laughter; but the very comicality of these illustrations aided to fasten his main conclusion in men's memories. In both these statements, imperfect as they were, great truths were embodied—truths which were sure to grow.

Lamarck's declaration, especially, that the development of organs is in ratio to their employment and his indications of the reproduction in progeny of what is gained or lost in parents by the influence of circumstances, entered as a most effective force into the development of the evolution theory.[5]

One of the imperfections in Lamarck's theory was that a giraffe, for example, was said to lengthen its neck by its exertion to reach high branches. Real evolution, on the other hand, comes from natural variation in species wherein the taller giraffe is better able to feed from higher branches and therefore more apt to survive and reproduce.

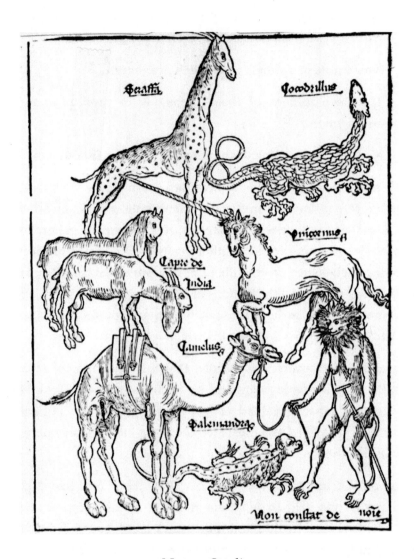

Nature Studies

Among the animals noted in a 1486 book entitled *Travels in the Holy Land* (captioned "these animals are accurately depicted as we saw them in the Holy Land") is a mythical unicorn.

(Smithsonian Institution Library)

However imperfect these beginning ideas of evolution, they were essentially different from the explanations of nature coming from theologians, who believed that the phoenix rising from its ashes proved the doctrine of the resurrection. Others believed that the mischief of monkeys proved that demons existed. Or that certain monkeys with no tails proved that Satan had been shorn of his glory. Finally, the weasel, with its erratic movements, was thought to be a type of the man estranged from the Word of God, who therefore could find no rest.

And then on July 1, 1858, two papers were presented at the Linnaean Society in London that were to change forever the notion that all species had been created instantaneously on or about 4004 BC, and had remained unchanged throughout time. The papers were from Alfred Russel Wallace and his friend Charles Darwin.

Darwin (1809-1882) had begun his investigation into plant and animal life in 1831, on his five-year voyage on the *Beagle*, but continued his work and the development of his theories for over twenty years before announcing them to the world. His friend, Wallace, had independently arrived at the same conclusion of evolution by natural selection on the basis of his own observations in the field. And when Darwin, to his astonishment, found in a letter from Wallace that they each had arrived at the same conclusion, it was amiably agreed to present their conclusions at a meeting of the Linnaean Society. The occasion passed without the slightest notice by anyone.

Darwin's *Origin of Species* was published a year later, in 1859, and revealed the three essential facts that were necessary to support the theory of evolution: (1) the struggle to exist, (2) the survival of the fittest, and (3) the factor of heredity. Bertrand Russell drew an interesting parallel in his book:

> Darwin's theory was essentially an extension to the animal
> and vegetable world of laisser-faire economics, and was suggested

by Malthus's theory of population. All living things reproduce themselves so fast that the greater part of each generation must die without having reached the age to leave descendants. A female cod-fish lays about 9,000,000 eggs a year. If all came to maturity and produced other cod-fish, the sea would, in a few years, give place to solid cod, while the land would be covered by a new deluge.[6]

Darwin had patiently withheld any announcement of the theory on which he had worked for over twenty years with an eye toward the controversy that such a theory would provoke. But even in 1859, in the *Origin of Species*, the only reference to the evolution of humans that Darwin allowed himself to make was the statement in his conclusion: "In the distant future I see open fields for far more important researches . . . Light will be thrown on the origin of man and his history."[7] It was not until 1871, when Darwin published *The Descent of Man*, that the prediction was realized. Here he proposed that humans appeared to have developed from apelike ancestors.

And then came the storm. Not since the Copernican revolution had science caused such consternation among the religious although it should be noted that not all of Darwin's antagonists were theologians. When the argument seemed to resolve itself down to the question of whether mankind had descended from the apes or the angels, the British statesman Benjamin Disraeli (1804-1881) declared, "I am on the side of the angels."

Of course, the theory of evolution was a surprise to most people and came as a particular shock to the religious who, for almost two thousand years, had a different view of creation. Certainly, the theory of evolution seemed to challenge the authenticity of the Bible (both of the Creation stories revealed in Genesis), diminish the intellectual and moral authority of the Church, and perhaps, represent an affront to the Creator himself. And this was evident from the outcries at the time:

- "The principle of natural selection is absolutely incompatible with the word of God" (Wilberforce, bishop of Oxford, Anglican Church).

- "A brutal philosophy—to wit, there is no God, and the ape is our Adam" (Cardinal Manning, an English Catholic).

- "If the Darwinian theory is true, Genesis is a lie, the whole framework of the book of life falls to pieces, and the revelation of God to man, as we Christians know it, is a delusion and a snare" (A theological authority).

- "If this hypothesis be true, then is the Bible an unbearable fiction . . . then have Christians for nearly two thousand years been duped by a monstrous lie" (An American theologian, Anglican Church).

- "A system which is repugnant at once to history, to the tradition of all peoples, to exact science, to observed facts, and even to Reason herself, would seem to need no refutation, did not alienation from God and the leaning toward materialism, due to depravity, eagerly see a support in all this tissue of fables" (Pope Pius IX).[8]

Criticisms such as these came from every corner of Christianity, but in time, religion was obliged to reconcile its views with Darwin's theory as it had with the Copernican theory and that of Galileo. The process, however, did not resolve itself easily or quickly. And there are still holdouts.

The holdouts, however, have recently been confronted by further evidence of our evolution from apelike ancestors. Science has shown that over 98 percent of the human genetic profile is still shared by chimps. This would seem to be a particular problem, inferentially, to those religionists who insist that man is made in the image of God.

Today, science accepts biological evolution and, along with it, the importance of cultural evolution. Stephen Jay Gould puts it in perspective:

> The evolutionary unity of humans with all other organisms is the cardinal message of Darwin's revolution for nature's most arrogant species.

> We are inextricably part of nature, but human uniqueness is not negated thereby. "Nothing but" an animal is as fallacious a statement as "created in God's own image." It is not mere hubris to argue that *Homo sapiens* is special in some sense—for each species is unique in its own way; shall we judge among the dance of the bees, the song of the humpback whale, and human intelligence?

> The impact of human uniqueness upon the world has been enormous because it has established a new kind of evolution to support the transmission across generations of learned knowledge and behavior. Human uniqueness resides primarily in our brains. It is expressed in the culture built upon our intelligence and the power it gives us to manipulate the world. Human societies change by cultural evolution, not as a result of biological alteration. We have no evidence for biological change in brain size or structure since *Homo sapiens* appeared in the fossil record some fifty thousand years ago. [Broca was right in stating that the cranial capacity of Cro-Magnon skulls was equal if not superior to ours.] All that we have done since then—the greatest transformation in the shortest time that our planet has experienced since its crust solidified nearly four billion years ago—is the product of cultural evolution. Biological [Darwinian] evolution continues in our species, but its rate, compared with cultural evolution, is so incomparably slow that its impact upon

An Ape Man

Darwin was ridiculed when he theorized in 1871 that man and ape shared a common ancestry. Today, evolution is widely accepted.

(Ardea London Ltd.)

the history of *Homo sapiens* has been small. While the gene for sickle-cell anemia declines in frequency among black Americans, we have invented the railroad, the automobile, radio and television, the atom bomb, the computer, the airplane and spaceship.[9]

So from a fascination with the heavens and all that goes on above us, humans had become interested in the earth and its secrets and then the human race and our evolution as a species. Perhaps it is more accurate to say that people became interested in everything at once when religion became less repressive. It is difficult to imagine the advances of science in the last several hundred years and, more so, to predict the advances of science in the centuries to come. The developments in chemistry and physics, for example, have been astonishing and are held in the highest regard today where in the Middle Ages, chemistry was regarded as a "devilish art" by the Christian church—although not without some justification, perhaps.

Notes

[1] Andrew Dickson White, *A History of the Warfare of Science with Theology in Christendom*, vol. 1 (New York: D. Appleton-Century, 1936), p. 55.

[2] Ibid., p. 54.

[3] Ibid., p. 58.

[4] Ibid., p. 45.

[5] Ibid., p. 62.

[6] Bertrand Russell, *Religion and Science* (New York: Oxford University Press, 1961), p. 72.

7   Charles Darwin, *Origin of Species* (New York: Collier, 1901), p. 314.

8   White, *A History of the Warfare of Science with Theology in Christendom*, vol. 1, p. 71.

9   Stephen Jay Gould, *The Mismeasure of Man* (New York: W. W. Norton, 1981), p. 324.

13

CHEMISTRY AND PHYSICS:
THAT OLD BLACK MAGIC

The Greek philosophers are often credited with providing an early impetus to the study of science, although philosophy was more concerned with reasoning and values while science looked to observation and exploration of the physical world. Socrates, it was noted, was concerned that investigations of certain physical phenomena were intrusions on the province of a divine authority. Plato's world of reason left little room (or need) for an interest in natural science, and Aristotle's concern for science included observations on what is true but centered more on speculations of what should be true.

But the contribution of these Greek philosophers was nevertheless considerable. Andrew Dickson White noted, "The impulse to human thought given by these great masters was of inestimable value to our race, and our legacy from them was especially precious—the idea that a science of Nature is possible, and that the highest occupation of man is the discovery of its laws. Still another gift from them was greatest of all, for they gave scientific freedom. They laid no interdict upon new paths; they interposed no barriers to the extension of knowledge; they threatened no doom in this life or in the next against investigators on new lines; they left the world free to seek any new methods and to follow any new paths which thinking men could find."[1]

The impetus given science by the Greek and Roman philosophers, however, was slowed by the coming of Christianity, and an interest in the natural world gave way to a concern about magic and the supernatural.

The early fathers of the Church had been outspoken about their belief in magic. Magicians were thought to derive their powers from devils—and devils were very much a part of the religious scene. Theologians in the Middle Ages developed their ideas about magic even further and continued to find support for their beliefs in the Bible: Satan was the prince of power in the air and so must be responsible for tempests; the devil afflicted Job with an illness, so devils were the cause of disease. And the stories of Nebuchadnezzar and Lot's wife showed that sorcerers could turn human beings into animals or even a pillar of salt.

Science as a whole suffered from its association with magic, but chemistry and physics, in particular, were susceptible to a presumed association with the black arts. In its early stage, alchemy was concerned with seeking the philosopher's stone, which would permit the transmutation of base metal to gold. Then alchemy became concerned with elixirs that would prolong life and cure disease by more or less magical means.

The Church responded to the threat of alchemy with a papal proclamation that at once warned the faithful and also showed that the pope himself had reason to fear the evil of sorcerers:

Thus the horror of magic and witchcraft increased on every hand, and in 1317 Pope John XXII issued his bull *Spondent Pariter*, leveled at the alchemists, but really dealing a terrible blow at the beginnings of chemical science. That many alchemists were

The Alchemist

Alchemy was originally concerned with seeking the philosopher's stone, which was said to turn base metals into gold. Martin Luther, among others, believed in the possibility.

(Mansell Collection/*Time Life*)

knavish is no doubt true, but no infallibility in separating the evil from the good was shown by the papacy in this matter. In this and in sundry other bulls and briefs we find Pope John, by virtue of his infallibility as the world's instructor in all that pertains to faith and morals, condemning real science and pseudo-science alike. In two of these documents, supposed to be inspired by wisdom from on high, he complains that both he and his flock are in danger of their lives by the arts of the sorcerers; he declares that such sorcerers can send devils into mirrors and finger rings, and kill men and women by a magic word; that they had tried to kill him by piercing a waxen image of him with needles in the name of the devil. He therefore called on all rulers, secular and ecclesiastical, to hunt down the miscreants who thus afflicted the faithful, and he especially increased the powers of inquisitors in various parts of Europe for this purpose. The impulse thus given to childish fear and hatred against the investigation of nature was felt for centuries; more and more chemistry came to be known as one of the "seven devilish arts."[2]

In the meantime, the blending of religion and magic produced a number of interesting ideas. One book recommended that the student who mixed chemicals should recite the psalm *Exsurge Domine* in the process and that certain chemical vessels be inscribed with Jesus's last words on the cross. A certain Vincent of Beauvais found support for an alchemical means of preserving life based on the biblical story of Noah fathering children when he was five hundred years old. The reality of the philosopher's stone (whereby base metals could be changed to gold) was proved by the words of St. John in Rev. 2:17, "To him that overcometh I will give a white stone." And the reasonableness of changing base metal into gold was supported by the Church's belief in the resurrection of the body; this analogy led Martin Luther to believe in the transmutation of metals.

The blending of religion and magic permeated most fields of knowledge during medieval times, and Christians and Jews vied with each other in giving the words, letters, and numbers found in scripture a mystical meaning. Mystical theories of numbers, for example, played a major part in shaping a medieval science:

> The sacred power of the number three was seen in the Trinity; in the three main divisions of the universe—the empyrean, the heavens, and the earth; in the three angelic hierarchies; in the three choirs of seraphim, cherubim, and thrones; in the three of dominions, virtues, and powers; in the three of principalities, archangels, and angels; in the three orders in the Church—bishops, priests, and deacons; in the three classes—the baptized, the communicants, and the monks; in the three degrees of attainment—light, purity, and knowledge; in the three theological virtues—faith, hope, and charity—and in much else. All this was brought into a theologico-scientific relation, then and afterward, with the three dimensions of space; with the three divisions of time—past, present, and future; with the three realms of the visible world—sky, earth, and sea; with the three constituents of man—body, soul, and spirit; with the threefold enemies of man—the world, the flesh, and the devil; with the three kingdoms in nature—mineral, vegetable, and animal.[3]

Apart from mystical numbers, the Church also had some novel ideas on the origin of natural gases. In ancient times, humans made some reasonably good guesses about the cause of gases found in mines. But Christendom brought a new theory that gave credit to the devil. St. Clement of Alexandria (c. 150-220) was one of the first to suppose that evil spirits were the cause of suffocating gases found in mines, caves, and wells.

Later, during the Reformation, a gentleman named Agricola divided the devils into two classes: first were the malignant imps who blew out the miners' lamps, and second were the friendly imps, who simply teased the miners in various ways. Attesting to the ways of the devils, Agricola noted a Saxon mine in Annaberg where a spirit destroyed twelve workmen by the power of his breath. Poof—and it was all over, according to this investigator. Finally, men such as the alchemist Basil Valentine began to uncover the truth about deadly gases and the matter was put to rest.

Andrew Dickson White traced a line extending from Galileo, Kepler, and Newton to Ohm, Faraday, and Helmholtz—all of whom helped to explain nature by a rule of natural law rather than by the capricious or vengeful acts of a spirit world. White says, "When Galileo dropped the differing weights from the Leaning Tower of Pisa, he began the end of Aristotelian authority in physics. When Torricelli balanced a column of mercury against a column of water and each of these against a column of air, he ended the theologic phrase that 'nature abhors a vacuum.' When Newton approximately determined the velocity of sound, he ended the theologic argument that we see the flash before we hear the roar because 'sight is nobler than hearing.' When Franklin showed that lightning is caused by electricity, and Ohm and Faraday proved that electricity obeys ascertained laws, they ended the theological idea of a divinity seated above the clouds and casting thunder bolts."[4]

And Franklin's lightning rod was to discredit a host of Church formulas used to combat the devil, or prince of power in the air, who also used lightning to strike at humans. It was said that the lightning rod did what exorcisms, and holy water, and processions, and the Agnus Dei, and the ringing of church bells, and the rack, and the burning of witches had failed to do.

Benjamin Franklin

Franklin's well-known experiment with a key and kite led to his invention of the lightning rod. He showed that lightning was a form of electricity and not the devil's hellfire.

(North Wind Picture Archives)

Notes

[1] Andrew Dickson White, *A History of the Warfare of Science with Theology in Christendom*, vol. 1 (New York: D. Appleton—Century, 1936), p. 374.

[2] Ibid., p. 383.

[3] Ibid., p. 396.

[4] Ibid., p. 407.

14

MEDICAL SCIENCE: A MISSING RIB

In earlier times, people held spirits responsible for events that could not otherwise be explained. Death and disease were no exceptions—both were thought to be caused by malignant spirits and, therefore, subject to the powers of the priest who dealt in such matters. History tells of the ancient priests in Egypt, Assyria, and Judea who claimed power over the spirits of disease as well as priests in the ancient civilizations of India, China, and Persia. The Old Testament and the New Testament contain many examples of bodily ills that were caused either by an angry god or a vengeful Satan.

Once again, reason began to break through in Greece where, five hundred years before Christ, the great Hippocrates (c. 460-377 BCE) rose above the superstitions of the times and established the foundation for a true medical science, although the development of a medical science was set back by a number of conflicting religious beliefs.

One obstacle was an acceptance of miracles that implied that a divine being, and perhaps only a divine being, could produce cures for certain ailments. A good case in point were the miracles attributed to Frances Xavier. As a missionary in India and Japan, Xavier (1506-1552) had never claimed miraculous powers, neither in conversation with his associates nor in the detailed accounts of his adventures, which he carefully committed to writing. But on his death, as sometimes happens in the case of religious figures, he was credited with curing the sick, casting out devils, and raising the dead—on quite a number of occasions.

For example, there was the matter of Xavier raising people from the dead. No mention of such a feat was made during Xavier's lifetime, neither in his own writing nor in the works of his contemporaries. But following Xavier's death, there began to appear accounts of his former ability to raise people from the dead. It began with a single such account and grew as various Christian writers told the story of Xavier's sainted life; at the time of his canonization, there were three such cases, and in a biography written by Father Bouhours some one hundred and thirty years after Xavier's death, the count had risen to fourteen. Numerous other healing legends attached to Xavier, and all such stories were to convince the faithful that religion could cure their ills.

Finally, Xavier was canonized by the same pope who condemned Galileo, Urban VIII, who was particularly impressed by reports that a crucifix, which Xavier had thrown on the waters to still a tempest, was later returned to him by a crab; that a lamp filled only with holy water burned brightly before an image of Xavier; and that Xavier reportedly had possessed the gift of tongues, enabling him to spread the *Word* across the lands of India and Japan. (St. Xavier's own accounts often spoke of the problems he encountered with foreign languages and spoke of a delay in a certain trip when the interpreter he had hired failed to show up.)

The cures attributed to Xavier and many other religious figures tended to confirm the popular belief that illness—and indeed death—were matters that could and, perhaps, should be handled by theology.

St. Augustine said, "All diseases of Christians are to be ascribed to their demons; chiefly do they torment fresh-baptized Christians, yea, even the guiltless newborn infants."[1] Other fathers of the Church declared that bodily pains were provoked by demons and that medicines were quite useless and, some thought, immoral. *OMG!*

As an outgrowth of this attitude, pastoral medicine came into vogue in the Middle Ages, resulting in huge revenues flowing into the coffers of churches throughout Europe and a spirited competition in the acquisition of relics thought to be efficacious in curing one or more diseases. Andrew Dickson White acknowledged that a "childlike faith" may have been responsible for the belief in the first place but that "a great development of the mercantile spirit" took place afterward:

> Enormous revenues flowed into various monasteries and churches in all parts of Europe from relics noted for their healing powers. Every cathedral, every great abbey, and nearly every parish church claimed possession of healing relics . . . . The commercial value of sundry relics was often very high. In the year 1056 a French ruler pledged securities in the amount of ten thousand solidi for the production of the relics of St. Just and St. Pastor . . . . The Emperor of Germany on one occasion demanded, as a sufficient pledge for the establishment of a city market, the arm of St. George.[2]

The belief in relics increased during the Middle Ages, and Bertrand Russell observed that "a belief in relics often survives exposure. For example, the bones of St. Rosalia, which are preserved in Palermo, have for many centuries been found effective in curing disease; but when examined by a profane anatomist they turned out to be the bones of a goat. Nevertheless the cures continued. We now know that certain kinds of diseases can be cured by faith, while others cannot; no doubt 'miracles' of healing do occur, but in an unscientific atmosphere legends soon magnify the truth, and obliterate the distinction between the hysterical diseases which can be cured in this way, and the others which demand a treatment based upon pathology."[3]

The competition for relics included legs, arms, skulls, and even the phallus of a St. Foutin, which was said to have powers to assist unfruitful women. One church covered its interior walls with the bones of St. Ursula and her eleven thousand virgin martyrs, although these were later found by anatomists to include the bones of men. The popes themselves offered a number of fetishes that, for a consideration, would protect the possessor from various maladies such as apoplexy, falling-sickness, and unexpected death. And it was to be expected that a reliance on fetish and miracle cures would have a dampening effect on legitimate scientific studies as the faithful were led to believe that religion, not medical science, was the answer to bodily ills. And the saints themselves were assigned specialties in the health care field. One prayed to St. Remy for relief from fever, St. Gall for tumors, St. Valentine for epilepsy, St. Christopher for sore throats, St. Ovid for deafness, St. Appollonia for toothaches, and St. Hubert for the bite of a mad dog. In fact, every country had a list of saints each of whom possessed special powers over some part of the body; all of which tended to make medical science irrelevant. But there were other obstacles, including a prohibition by the church on dissecting the bodies of the dead. Anatomists were regarded by the church fathers as butchers who, in their meddling with a body, might forfeit the hope of resurrection for the body involved. The abhorrence of dissection extended as well to surgery, which, for over a thousand years, was thought to be a dishonorable pursuit.

The Christian approach to medicine took a number of turns, one of the strangest of which was to provoke the demons inhabiting the diseased body with degrading substances—and so the patient would consume medicine made from "the livers of toads, the blood of frogs and rats, fibres of the hangman's rope, and ointment made from the body of gibbetted criminals."[4]

Another medical misdirection wrought by the Church was the doctrine of signatures, which supposed that the Almighty had made his sign on certain substances to alert people to their curative powers: "Hence it was held that bloodroot, on account of its red juice is good for the blood; liverwort, having a leaf like the liver, cures diseases of the liver; eyebright, being marked with a spot like an eye, cures diseases of the eye; celandine, having a yellow juice, cures jaundice; bugloss, resembling a snake's head, cures snakebite; red flannel, looking like blood, cures blood taints, and therefore rheumatism; bear's grease, being taken from an animal thickly covered with hair, is recommended to persons fearing baldness."[5] Spittle was not a signature substance, as such, but was believed to have curative powers based on the reference in the fourth Gospel to Jesus's use of spittle.

The shrine cures were another Christian phenomenon. Certain lakes, springs, and other spots were thought to be sacred, where miracles of healing happened. Still today, many people believe in the healing powers resident in certain locations throughout the world.

Protestantism contributed its own marvelous cure by proclaiming that the royal touch could cure diseases, especially epilepsy and scrofula. And there is probably no better-documented idea in the history of miracle healing than the reports that the touch of a king or queen effected the cure of some disease. England's Charles II reportedly touched over one hundred thousand people, and his miraculous cures were duly reported by His Majesty's surgeon in a published account.

In the midst of these superstitions, medical science had a number of heroes, one of whom was Andreas Vesalius (1514-1564), founder of the science of anatomy. It was Vesalius who risked the charge of sacrilege, the perils of the plague, and popular opinion to dissect dead bodies and produce his great illustrated work on human anatomy. And with it, he raised a number of interesting questions: For one, he found no bone in the body (as theologians believed existed) that was incorruptible and served as the basis for the regrowth, or resurrection, of the body after death. For another, he found that men had an equal number of ribs on each side of their bodies—not (as theologians then believed) that men had been missing a rib ever since the Almighty took it from Adam to create Eve.

In another skirmish between religion and science, theologians condemned the use of innoculations in the eighteenth century as "flying in the face of Providence" and "endeavoring to baffle a Divine judgment."[6] It was held, for example, that smallpox was "a judgment of God on the sins of the people" and thus should not be acted against. For did not Hosea say, "He hath torn, and he will heal us; he hath smitten, and he will bind us up"?

Anesthetics provided another occasion for the intervention of theology. In 1847, the recommended use of anesthetics in childbirth was argued against by the clergy who quoted God's words to Eve: "In sorrow shalt thou bring forth children" (Gen. 3:16). And so for women in childbirth, anesthetics were thought to fly in the face of providence. Fortunately for men, God had placed Adam in a deep sleep when extracting his rib, and thus, anesthetics might be given to men without the risk of divine censure.

Just as the Christian church had held that smallpox was a divine judgment, it believed that the other great plagues of history served a divine purpose—the punishment of sinners. There was a basis in history for such a belief as Greece and Rome had also attributed plagues to the anger of the Gods, and the children of Israel believed that epidemics were manifestations of a divine will. So people could only look to themselves and their sins when, in the middle of the fourteenth century, the black death swept away more than half the population of England and over 25 million people throughout Europe.

The main cause of these epidemics was, of course, poor sanitary conditions. Descriptions of life at the time suggested that "down to the sixteenth and seventeenth centuries the filthiness in the ordinary mode

Outstanding among the innovators was Andreas Vesalius (1514-1564), who was professor at Padua. Vesalius carried out some unprecedentedly scrupulous dissections and used the latest in artistic techniques and printing for the more than 200 woodcuts in his "On the Structure of the Human Body" (1543). Originally himself a Galenist, Vesalius became a leading figure in the revolt against Galen's teachings.

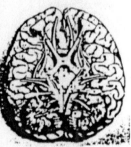

Body by Vesalius

Andreas Vesalius was a professor at Padua and a noted innovator. He discovered that men were not missing a rib, which the clergy believed was removed when the Almighty created Eve.

(Royal College of Surgeons)

of life in England was such as we can now hardly conceive: fermenting organic material was allowed to accumulate and become a part of the earthen floors of rural dwellings . . . . Men were confined in dungeons rarely if ever disinfected after the death of previous occupants, and on corridors connecting directly with the foulest sewers; there was no proper disinfection, ventilation or drainage."[7] And the result was that cholera, smallpox, and typhoid fever raged throughout Europe for centuries.

The religious reaction to such calamities took several forms. Chapels were built to saints who were thought to be effective in curbing the outbreak of cholera and other epidemics, images of the Virgin Mary were paraded through streets, and fetishes of all sorts were employed by the faithful. In the thirteenth and fourteenth centuries, processions of flagellants marched through Europe, reciting psalms and scourging their bodies. Also unfortunately, some Christians thought that Jews or witches were to blame, and thousands of people were tortured and burned, presumably to win the favor of the Almighty—all in keeping with the biblical injunction that "Thou shall not suffer a witch to live" (Exod. 22:18).

And so the Church authorities, instead of looking to medicine and improved sanitation, looked to atonement and made no effort to clean up their own act as it were:

> And here certain theological reasonings came in to resist the evolution of a proper sanitary theory. Out of the Orient had been poured into the thinking of western Europe the theological idea that the abasement of man adds to the glory of God; that indignity to the body may secure salvation to the soul; hence, that cleanliness betokens pride and filthiness humility. Living in filth was regarded by great numbers of holy men, who set an example to the Church and to society, as an evidence of sanctity. St. Jerome and the Breviary of the Roman Church dwell with unction on the

fact that St. Hilarion lived his whole life long in utter physical uncleanliness; St. Athanasius glorifies St. Anthony because he had never washed his feet; St. Abraham's most striking evidence of holiness was that for fifty years he washed neither his hands nor his feet; St. Sylvia never washed any part of her body save her fingers. St. Euphraxia belonged to a convent in which the nuns religiously abstained from bathing; St. Mary of Egypt was eminent for filthiness; St. Simon Stylites was in this respect unspeakable—the least that can be said is that he lived in ordure and stench intolerable to his visitors. The Lives of the Saints dwell with complacency on the statement that, when sundry Eastern monks showed a disposition to wash themselves, the Almighty manifested his displeasure by drying up a neighbouring stream until the bath which it had supplied was destroyed.[8]

Treatment of Insanity

From the early days of Greece and Rome, it appeared that the treatment of insanity was developing in a constructive manner. The great Hippocrates, in the fifth century before Christ, had believed that madness was simply a disease of the brain, and the weight of his opinion influenced thought for centuries to come. In the first two centuries after Christ, Aretaeus and Soranus developed new data along the same lines; further thoughts about the treatment of the insane were developed by Galen and Aurelianus before the third century had ended. Through the seventh century, learning continued to develop the idea that insanity was a disease of the brain and should be treated with gentleness and kindness.

But then theologic opinion changed beliefs on the cause and treatment of the insane when "there set into the early Church a current of belief which was destined to bring all these noble acquisitions of science and religion to naught, and, during centuries, to inflict tortures, physical and mental, upon hundreds of thousands of innocent men and women—a belief which held its cruel sway for nearly eighteen centuries; and this belief was that madness was mainly or largely possession by the devil."[9]

The basis for the idea of a diabolical agency began in the sacred literature of Orientals, and their formulae for removing evil spirits was picked up, in turn, in the holy books of the Jews and Christians, along with many other ancient beliefs. Plato too contributed to the notion of a satanic influence affecting the mentally disturbed. And "this belief took firm hold upon the strongest men. The case of St. Gregory the Great is typical. He was a pope of exceedingly broad mind for his time, and no one will think him unjustly reckoned one of the four Doctors of the Western Church. Yet he solemnly relates that a nun, having eaten some lettuce without making the sign of the cross, swallowed a devil, and that, when commanded by a holy man to come forth, the devil replied: 'How am I to blame? I was sitting on the lettuce, and this woman, not having made the sign of the cross, ate me along with it.'"[10]

One of the prescriptions to cure the insane was to brew up a drink with clear ale, sing seven masses over it, add garlic and holy water, and let the possessed sing the *Beati Immaculati*. But a *Treasury of Exorcisms* gave numerous prescriptions for casting out the devils:

- Insults were hurled at the demons by calling them rude names, such as envious crocodile, swollen toad, loathsome cobbler, sooty spirit from Tartarus, lustful and stupid one, and more.

- Scare tactics employed the use of ponderous language and imported Greek and Hebrew names that were sure to impress the demons: Tetragrammaton, Athanatos, Schemhamphora.

- Drugs and substances with objectionable odors were burned under the nose of the afflicted so that the sulphurous fumes, for example, would offend the demon.

- Likenesses of the devil were subject to the humiliation of being spat upon and trampled—and by persons of very low social stature.

- And of course, curses were hurled at the demons that reminded them of the great powers of their Christian adversary: "May Agyos strike thee, as he did Egypt, with frogs."

The efficacy of such procedures in driving out demons was undeniable, and many devils and imps surrendered to the Church. The Jesuit fathers in Vienna, in 1583, counted over 12,652 living devils that had been cast out, and throughout the Middle Ages, the Church boasted of a widespread success against Satan:

For hundreds of years this idea of diabolic possession was steadily developed. It was believed that devils entered into animals, and animals were accordingly exorcised, tried, tortured, convicted, and executed. The great St. Ambrose tells us that a priest, while saying mass, was troubled by the croaking of frogs in a neighbouring marsh; that he exorcised them, and so stopped their noise. St. Bernard, as the monkish chroniclers tell us, mounting the pulpit to preach in his abbey, was interrupted by a cloud of flies; straightway the saint uttered the sacred formula of excommunication, when the flies fell dead upon the pavement in heaps, and were cast out with shovels! A formula of exorcism attributed to a saint of the ninth century, which remained in use down to a recent period, especially declares insects injurious to crops to be possessed of evil spirits, and names, among the animals to be excommunicated or exorcised, mice, moles, and serpents. The use of exorcism against caterpillars and grasshoppers was also common. In the thirteenth century a Bishop of Lausanne, finding that the eels in Lake Leman troubled the fishermen, attempted to remove the difficulty by exorcism, and two centuries later one of his successors excommunicated all the May-bugs in the diocese. As late as 1731 there appears an entry on the Municipal Register of Thonon as follows: *"Resolved,* That this town join with other parishes of this province in obtaining from Rome an excommunication against the insects, and that it will contribute *pro rata* to the expenses of the same."[11]

Many of the insane suffered harsh tortures and confinement. As late as the sixteenth century, the bodies of lunatics were scourged to drive out demons, and throughout Europe, there existed witch towers for the torture of the insane and fool towers, where the more gentle lunatics were imprisoned. So there were many forms of insanity, and the treatment varied by degree. When the disease took a milder form, the subject of it was sometimes treated with reverence, and some patients were even elevated to sainthood: such examples as St. Francis of Assissi and St. Catherine of Siena in Italy, St. Bridget in Sweden, St. Theresa in Spain, St. Mary Alacoque in France, and Louise Lateau in Belgium were typical. But some cases shocked public feeling and were treated with harsh measures. In the case of Simon Marin, who in his insanity believed himself to be the son of God, the Church acted to have him burned alive at Paris and his ashes scattered over the land.

Theories abounded on how possession took place, and the Christian beliefs were similar to those held by many ancient races and societies. Satan could be swallowed while eating food (as in the guise of an insect on a leaf of lettuce) or could be breathed in through nose or mouth or enter the body through other orifices as the person slept. Some divines took special care during exorcisms that the evil imp did not jump from the mouth of the afflicted into their own.

So medical science was hampered by Christian superstitions relating to good and evil spirits. The good spirits were thought to be both capable and caring, which made medical science unnecessary and perhaps an affront to our invisible benefactors. The evil spirits served to explain the failure of the good spirits to remedy our ailments and provided a continuing raison d'être for religion. In effect, the parish priest served as scientist and physician, and in his black bag were all that was needed to remedy the ills of humankind. In *Religion and Science,* Bertrand Russell had a concluding thought on medical science:

> But although, as we have just seen, theology still tries to interfere in medicine where moral issues are supposed to be specially involved, yet over most of the field the battle for the scientific independence of medicine has been won. No one now thinks it impious to avoid pestilences and epidemics by sanitation and hygiene; and though some still maintain that diseases are sent by God, they do not argue that it is therefore impious to try to avoid them. The consequent improvement in health and increase in longevity is one of the most remarkable and admirable characteristics of our age. Even if science had done nothing else for human happiness, it would deserve our gratitude on this account. Those who believe in the utility of theological creeds would have difficulty in pointing to any comparable advantage that they have conferred upon the human race.[13]

Notes

1   Andrew Dickson White, *A History of the Warfare of Science with Theology in Christendom,* vol. 2 (New York: D. Appleton—Century, 1936), p. 27.

2   Ibid., p. 28.

3   Bertrand Russell, *Religion and Science* (New York: Oxford University Press, 1961), p. 83.

4   White, *A History of the Warfare of Science with Theology in Christendom*, p. 79.

5   Ibid., p. 38.

6   Ibid., p. 56.

7   Ibid., p. 82.

8   Ibid., p. 69.

9   Ibid., p. 99.

10   Ibid., p. 101.

11   Ibid., p. 113.

12   Ibid., p. 164.

13   Russell, *Religion and Science*, p. 108.

15

The Bible: A Textbook on Science

Holy books are a fundamental part of every religion. Along with the traditions of the priesthood, it is the holy book that provides a lasting description of the god and his intentions as well as his instructions to the faithful. Some religions view their holy book as the literal words of a god while others believe their book is inspired by a god, although written by men and women. Whichever the interpretation, historically, the contents of the books are unassailable in the eyes of the faithful and not subject to doctrinal error or historical inaccuracy.

Of course, as religion itself was born of societies over ten thousand years ago, so were many holy books written in ancient cultural settings, given to the fanciful stories of their time, and inhibited by a lack of knowledge available to more contemporary cultures. So the holy books were the thoughts of people who believed in mythical heroes, marauding spirits, and magic in its many forms. Sticks could be turned into snakes, demons concealed in human bodies, people returned from the dead, and lightning called down from on high. And paradise beckoned, with winged angels to welcome the virtuous to a condition of eternal bliss—or so it was believed by the faithful.

For almost two thousand years, Christians in all walks of life took the Bible to be literally true. Whatever their educational background or personal experience, people believed that the Bible was the literal Word of God and therefore not subject to question or challenge. Did Jonah live in the body of a great fish? Was Eve created from Adam's rib? Would the world's animals fit into a homemade ark? Was there really a magic garden and a talkative snake? The answer was yes if it said so in the Bible—or if theologians so interpreted the words of the Bible.

The literal interpretation of the Bible necessarily gave rise to many mistaken views of the universe. And a young science was often frustrated by the Church's insistence that any new findings support the teachings of the Bible. In fact, there was little science of any kind because the Church undertook to answer all questions concerning the nature of the universe by recourse to its holy book. Thus a sacred science was created, and the Bible was viewed as the only valid source of knowledge. As noted, St. Augustine (354-430 CE) gave words to this belief in his declaration: "Nothing is to be accepted save on the authority of Scripture, since greater is that authority than all the powers of the human mind."

St. Augustine's message was a clear statement of the Church's belief that all truth and knowledge flowed from the Bible, which had been vested with these qualities by a holy ghost. And for more than a thousand years thereafter, the Church resisted any ideas that did not conform to scripture and enhance the authority of the Church. Thus were scientists like Copernicus, Galileo, and others frustrated in their attempts to explain natural phenomena by natural causes.

Today scholars recognize many inconsistencies in the Bible, beginning with the early history of humans as recounted in Genesis. For example, one account of Genesis spoke of the six days of Creation, each with a morning and an evening, and a daily record of accomplishment.

The second account of Genesis spoke of a single day only with Creation as an instantaneous act.

In his book *Folklore in the Old Testament*, Sir James Frazer notes a "striking discrepancy" between the two accounts of the creation of man in the first and second chapters of Genesis: "In the first narrative the deity begins with fishes and works steadily up through birds and beasts to man and woman. In the second narrative he begins with man and works downward through the lower animals to woman, who apparently marks the nadir of divine workmanship."[1]

And so Frazer notes the order of merit is reversed, and in the second version, woman is fashioned as a mere afterthought and from a rib taken while Adam was asleep. The discrepancy between the two versions may be ascribed to indifferent editing, which failed to note the obvious contradiction of the two accounts. Noteworthy also, in the Jehovistic document, is the author's attitude toward woman, who Frazer suggests "hardly attempts to hide his deep contempt for woman. The lateness of her creation and the irregular and undignified manner of it—made out of a piece of her lord and master, after all the lower animals had been created in a regular and decent manner—sufficiently mark the low opinion he held of her nature; and in the sequel his misogynism, as we may fairly call it, takes a still darker tinge, when he ascribes all the misfortunes and sorrows of the human race to the credulous folly and unbridled appetite of its first mother."[2]

We may take it, then, that the Bible opens on two conflicting accounts of Creation, a concern which is only heightened by the failure of the editor to acknowledge the discrepancy. In the second account, moreover, the author appears to be a misogynist, whose views were given standing by their inclusion in the Bible, with a consequence that women have been a casualty of his thinking ever since.

Beyond the errors and inconsistencies that have been found in the Bible, scholarship has revealed that many of its stories come from folklore. An example cited by Frazer is the biblical conception that man was modeled out of clay as a figure might be modeled by a potter. This conception of man's creation was shared by a number of earlier religions as Frazer notes, "From various allusions in Babylonian literature it would seem that the Babylonians also conceived man to have been moulded out of clay . . . In Egyptian mythology Khnoumou, the father of the Gods, is said to have moulded man out of clay on his potter's wheel . . . So in Greek legend the sage Prometheus is said to have moulded the first men out of clay at Panopeus in Phocis."[3] And Frazer goes on to conclude that "such rude conceptions of the origin of mankind, common to Greeks, Hebrews, Babylonians, and Egyptians, were handed down to the civilized peoples of antiquity by their early or barbarous forefathers. In fact, tribes from the Pacific islands, Asia, Africa and even America shared the belief that the first man must have been moulded from clay."[4]

So the Bible does not offer an original concept of man's creation, but merely relies on the folklore that was extant. The idea of a creation out of clay no doubt arose because, in earlier days, people were unable to visualize their gods in terms other than their own recognized abilities—and so their gods must have modeled shapes from clay as they themselves were wont to do. And yet Christianity accepted the story as literal truth, and for the better part of two thousand years.

One of the best-known stories in the Bible, that of Adam and Eve, also came to the Old Testament by way of ancient folklore. The same symbolism of a magic garden and talking serpent was seen in the earliest cuneiform texts, shown on Sumerian cylinder seals, and recounted in the folklore of earlier people long before the biblical account of Adam and Eve. The purpose of the Fall legend throughout the world was simply to explain the existence of evil and human suffering in a world supposedly under the protection of a beneficent god. The Fall made humanity accountable for the problems in the world and, thereby, preserved the image of a capable and caring Creator. The consequences were far-reaching for Adam, Eve, and others as Frazer summarized in the following:

> And learning from the abashed couple how they had disobeyed his command by eating of the fruit of the tree of knowledge, he flew into a towering passion. He cursed the serpent, condemning him to go on his belly, to eat dust, and to be the enemy of mankind all the days of his life: he cursed the ground, condemning it to bring forth thorns and thistles; he cursed the woman, condemning her to bear children in sorrow and to be in subjection to her husband: he cursed the man, condemning him to wring his daily bread from the ground in the sweat of his brow, and finally to return to the dust out of which he had been taken. Having relieved his feelings by these copious maledictions, the irascible but really kind-hearted deity relented so far as to make coats of skins for the culprits to replace their scanty apron of fig-leaves; and clad in these new garments the shamefaced pair retreated among the trees, while in the west the sunset died away and the shadows deepened on Paradise Lost.[5]

Remarkably, the story of Adam and Eve was credited as literal truth until the middle of the twentieth century. It is now viewed by scholars as an ancient myth and perhaps instructional on that level.

In its symbolism, the particular story of the serpent and the magic garden has been found in folklore around the world although there were also other settings that served to explain the problems of life. The prophet Zoroaster preached a Fall in the ancient Persian religion and Greek mythology also had its legend of a Fall. Clearly, many cultures have had difficulty in reconciling the ills of the world with the goodness of their gods and were left with no real alternative than to absolve the gods and shoulder the blame.

Another curiosity in the Old Testament concerns the mark of Cain. In Genesis, after Cain murdered his brother Abel, he became an outcast, but his remonstrations with God were rewarded with a distinctive mark that protected him from assailants. This may have derived from the mark many tribal members wore as a protection, as it signified that their death would surely be avenged by their tribe. Frazer speculated that, in this case, the mark may have been a protection against his brother's ghost, for "this explanation of the mark of Cain has the advantage of relieving the Biblical narrative from a manifest absurdity. For on the usual interpretation God affixed the mark to Cain in order to save him from human assailants, apparently forgetting that there was nobody to assail him, since the earth was as yet inhabited only by the murderer himself and his parents. Hence, by assuming that the foe of whom the first murderer went in fear was a ghost instead of a living man, we avoid the irreverence of imparting the deity a grave lapse of memory little in keeping with divine omniscience."[6]

The legend of the great flood in the book of Genesis once again reveals two different versions of the account, marked by inconsistencies, which were later combined to form a single story. One version noted a distinction between clean and unclean animals of those invited aboard while the other writer made no such distinction. One version suggested that the flood lasted sixty-one days; the other noted a duration of twelve months and ten days. In one account, the flood was caused by rain; in the other, both rain and water from subterranean sources were responsible. An altar and sacrifice were mentioned in one version but not the other.

Moreover, it was found that the Hebrew story was apparently taken from a Babylonian flood story, which preceded the Hebrew account by eleven or twelve centuries. Frazer noted,

A very cursory comparison of the Hebrew with the Babylonian account of the Deluge may suffice to convince us that the two narratives are not independent, but that one of them must be derived from the other, or both from a common original. The points of resemblance between the two are far too numerous and detailed to be accidental. In both narratives the divine powers resolve to destroy mankind by a great flood; in both the secret is revealed beforehand to a man by a god, who directs him to build a great vessel, in which to save himself and seed of every kind. It is probably no mere accidental coincidence that in the Babylonian story, as reported by Berosus, the hero saved from the flood was the tenth King of Babylon, and that in the Hebrew story Noah, was the tenth man in descent from Adam. In both narratives the favoured man, thus warned of God, builds a huge vessel in several stories, makes it water-tight with pitch or bitumen, and takes into it his family and animals of all sorts: in both, the deluge is brought about in large measure by heavy rain, and lasts for a greater or less number of days: in both, all mankind are drowned except the hero and his family: in both, the man sends forth birds, a raven and a dove, to see whether the water of the flood has abated: in both, the dove after a time returns to the ship because it could find no place in which to rest: in both, the raven does not return: in both, the vessel at last grounds on a mountain: in both, the hero, in gratitude for his rescue, offers sacrifice on the mountain: in both, the gods smell the sweet savour, and their anger is appeased.[7]

Following the account reported in Genesis, other adornments to the story were conceived by the Hebrews. It was said that, prior to the flood, people led a life of consummate ease, wherein one sowing would produce a harvest that would last forty years, wherein magic arts could compel the sun and moon to do the Hebrew's bidding, and wherein children were in their mother's womb only a few days, and after birth, they could immediately walk, talk, and fend off demons. It was also said that God warned the Hebrews of an impending punishment by having the sun rise in the west and set in the east for a seven-day period. These, and other embellishments to the flood story, illustrate the proclivity to enhance the narrative for popular consumption as indeed many Bible stories were punctuated with miraculous happenings.

Finally, Frazer reports that similar stories of floods were rampant in the ancient world and among earlier peoples, all thought to be the work of the gods and many sharing the same elements as the Hebrew story and the earlier Babylonian legend from which it was taken. The Babylonian legend itself appears to have been derived from a still more ancient Sumerian legend. And so the story in Genesis was far from original in the telling.

So although the Bible was once held to be infallible and the only valid source of knowledge, it is now apparent that the Old Testament was a very human undertaking with a generous measure of editing errors and other inconsistencies in the material. And many of the stories which formed the basis for our religious beliefs and explained the human condition overall were not original but myths adopted from ancient civilizations or early peoples. The stories of Creation, Adam and Eve, and the great deluge are representative of the many Bible stories that were dipped from the vast reservoir of ancient religious myth.

At the least, it seems apparent that many questions are still to be answered with respect to the origins and authorship of biblical narratives. And there is no doubt that the Old Testament included a large measure of myth in its recountals. Certainly, neither the Old Testament nor the New Testament could be taken as authoritative in the sense intended by St. Augustine, who believed that the Holy Ghost had vouchsafed the truth, accuracy, and authority of the Bible.

There is another perspective on holy books, however. They may be honored, if not for their scientific accuracy, then for the insights they provide on the development of human thought. Andrew Dickson White wrote this about science and holy scripture:

> Science, while conquering them, had found in our Scriptures a far nobler truth than that literal historical exactness for which theologians have so long and so vainly contended. More and more as we consider the results of the long struggle in this field we are brought to the conclusion that the inestimable value of the great sacred books of the world is found in their revelation of the steady striving of our race after higher conceptions, beliefs, and aspirations, both in morals and religion. Unfolding and exhibiting this long-continued effort, each of the great sacred books of the world is precious, and all, in the highest sense, are true. Not one of them, indeed, conforms to the measure of what mankind has now reached in historical and scientific truth; to make a claim to such conformity is folly, for it simply exposes those who make it and the books for which it is made to loss of their just influence.

> That to which the great sacred books of the world conform, and our own most of all, is the evolution of the highest conceptions, beliefs, and aspirations of our race from its childhood through the great turning points in its history. Herein lies the truth of all bibles, and especially of our own. Of vast value they indeed often are as a record of historical outward fact; recent researches in the East are constantly increasing this value; but it is not for this that we prize them most: They are eminently precious, not as a record of outward fact, but as a mirror of the evolving heart, mind, and soul of man.[10]

The Deluge

Like a number of Bible stories, the tale of Noah and the ark was taken from a Babylonian story that, in turn, was derived from an ancient Sumerian legend.

(Erich Lessing/Art Resource)

As holy books embody "the deepest searchings into the most vital problems of humanity in all its stages: the naive guesses of the world's childhood, the opening conceptions of its youth, the more fully rounded beliefs of its maturity," they may be studied with profit, but with an understanding that history and myth are intermingled and that many of the stories are apocryphal. Wars, persecutions, and prejudices have all been justified—engendered—by statements in the Bible, just as scripture has been the source of humanity's loftiest sentiments.

Then maybe George and Ira Gershwin had it right when they said,

> It ain't necessarily so,
> De t'ings dat yo' li'ble
> To read in de Bible,
> It ain't necessarily so.
> (*Porgy and Bess*)*

[handwritten: the things that you belief to read in the Bible It aint necessarily so.]

Notes

1 Sir James G. Frazer, *Folklore in the Old Testament*, abridged ed. (New York: Avenel Books, 1988), p. 1.

2 Ibid., p. 2.

3 Ibid., p. 3.

4 Ibid., p. 4.

5 Ibid., p. 15.

6 Ibid., p. 45.

7 Ibid., p. 62.

8 "Who Wrote the Bible?" *U.S. News & World Report*, December 10, 1990, p. 63.

9 Robert W. Funk and Roy W. Hoover, *The Five Gospels: The Search for the Authentic Words of Jesus* (New York: Macmillan Publishing, 1993).

10 Andrew Dickson White, *A History of the Warfare of Science with Theology in Christendom*, vol. 1 (New York: D. Appleton-Century, 1936), p. 22.

16

PHILOLOGY: THE LANGUAGE IN PARADISE

Philology was the science that finally demolished the Tower of Babel, which, according to the legend, had first been destroyed by the Almighty when he jealously noted that humans were building a tower so high that it was in danger of encroaching on his own preserve—not that far above. And so the Almighty confounded the builders of the Tower of Babel by giving them different languages so they could not understand each other and then proceeded to scatter them about the face of the earth. que Hde P.

And the whole earth was of one language, and of one speech.

And it came to pass, as they journeyed from the east, that they found a plain in the land of Shinar; and they dwelt there.

And they said one to another, Go to, let us make brick, and burn them thoroughly. And they had brick for stone, and slime had they for mortar.

And they said, Go to, let us build us a city, and a tower, whose top may reach unto heaven; and let us make a name, lest we be scattered abroad upon the face of the whole earth.

And the Lord came down to see the city and the tower, which the children of men builded.

And the Lord said, Behold, the people is one, and they have all one language; and this they begin to do: and now nothing will be restrained from them, which they have imagined to do.

Go to, let us go down, and there confound their language, that they may not understand one another's speech.

So the Lord scattered them abroad from thence upon the face of all the earth: and they left off to build the city.

Therefore is the name of it called Babel; because the Lord did there confound the language of all the earth: and from thence did the Lord scatter them abroad upon the face of all the earth." (Gen. 6:1-9)

As it happened, however, the Hebrew explanation of the origin of language was found to have been told in detail by the Chaldeans, who predated the Hebrews—and probably in connection with a specific tower that the Chaldeans had built for astronomical observations but whose faulty construction had caused it to topple over before completion; the Chaldeans had chosen to believe it was the work of a jealous god.

So the Chaldeans and then the Hebrews accounted for the diversity of language on the earth, not by the evolution of tongues, but by the act of a jealous god. Similarly, Hindu legends explained the confusion of tongues by Brahma cutting down the knowledge tree when the tree rose so high in the heavens as to threaten his private heaven; he proceeded to cut the branches and scatter them, and the remnants grew again as different languages and customs scattered over the earth. Mexicans accounted for differences in language by a legend that the gods resented the great Pyramid of Cholula, which reached so far into the heavens that it angered the gods who broke it down, whereafter every separate family received a language of its own.

Philology answered other questions about language as well. In a very human way, many different cultures assumed that their language was the very first language and usually a god-given language. So the Chaldeans believed their language came from the god Oannes, the Egyptians from their god Thoth, and the Hebrews from their god Yahweh. The Hebrews assumed that everyone spoke their language—Yahweh in his talks with Adam and even the serpent in its conversations with Eve.

So the idea of language was a natural concomitant to other beliefs in exclusivity. For the most part, all ancient nations believed they were chosen or favored by their god, that their deity was superior to all other, that their city was actually the center of the earth. Today, when we know that language differs as part of a natural growth process in various parts of the world, we may be surprised that for over two thousand years, it was believed that the Almighty spoke Hebrew and gave that language to humanity, later creating a diversity of language by destroying the Tower of Babel.

The idea of the diversity of language can be explained by the propensity of people to assign unknown causes to a spirit world and to construct a story around the event to facilitate human consumption:

> The "law of wills and causes," formulated by Comte, was exemplified here as in so many other cases. That law is, that, when men do not know the natural causes of things, they simply attribute them to wills like their own; thus they obtain a theory which provisionally takes the place of science, and this theory forms a basis for theology.

The Tower of Babel

Many cultures around the world have believed that the diversity of languages was caused by a jealous god—the Chaldeans, Hebrews, Hindu, Mexicans, and ancient Greeks, among others.

(The British Library)

Examples of this recur to any thinking reader of history. Before the simpler laws of astronomy were known, the sun was supposed to be trundled out into the heavens every day and the stars hung up in the firmament every night by the right hand of the Almighty. Before the laws of comets were known, they were thought to be missiles hurled by an angry God at a wicked world. Before the real cause of lightning was known, it was supposed to be the work of a good God in his wrath, or of evil spirits in their malice. Before the laws of meteorology were known, it was thought that rains were caused by the Almighty or his angels opening "the windows of heaven" to let down upon the earth "the waters that be above the firmament." Before the laws governing physical health were known, diseases were supposed to result from the direct interposition of the Almighty or of Satan. Before the laws governing mental health were known, insanity was generally thought to be diabolic possession. All these early conceptions were naturally embodied in the sacred books of the world, and especially in our own.

So, in this case, to account for the diversity of tongues, the direct intervention of the Divine Will was brought in. As this diversity was felt to be an inconvenience, it was attributed to the will of a Divine Being in anger. To explain this anger, it was held that it must have been provoked by human sin.

Out of this conception explanatory myths and legends grew as thickly and naturally as elms along water-courses; of these the earliest form known to us is found in the Chaldean accounts, and nowhere more clearly than in the legend of the Tower of Babel.[1]

The Chaldeans and the Hebrews chose a tower for their language myth simply because, in ancient times, it was assumed that gods lived above the clouds and people wished to build their altars as near to the gods as possible, just as the Hindu had chosen a high tree and the Mexicans, the great Pyramid of Cholula. And all attributed a jealous nature to their god, which ultimately put humans in their place—a lower and less-exalted position.

Plato was one who knew the dangers of human pride. We are told that Plato believed that in a golden age, long ago, humans and beasts spoke the same language, but Zeus confounded their speech because humans were proud and were even presumptuous enough to ask for eternal youth and immortality.

But if the origin of language is clear to us now, it was just as clear to the early fathers of the Church that Hebrew was the first language and that other languages followed the intercession of the Almighty at the Tower of Babel. Origen believed it, St. Jerome and St. Augustine believed it and further believed that—beyond the language, as such—the words, letters, and even the punctuation in the Bible had been passed down by the Almighty.

It was on this last point, a matter of punctuation, that religion and science had its first skirmish. The punctuation in question was the vowel points in the Hebrew language, which were discovered to have first been used sometime after the second century. And this was difficult to reconcile with the idea that God had given humans the Hebrew language (vowel points included) at the creation of the universe. It was, in fact, thought that God had pulled Adam aside and, during a walk in the garden, had personally coached him in the Hebrew language.

It was from this lesson in language that Adam was able to name all the animals that were brought before him by Jehovah, thought by the clergy to be an amazing exploit. There was, however, a troubling exception to Adam's roster of animal life because fish were not specifically mentioned in the biblical account. Some theologians noted the difficulties that would have been encountered in bringing fish into the Garden of Eden to receive their names, but others had faith that the Almighty could easily have brought them to the garden for this purpose. The Hebrew names of all living creatures, except possibly fishes, became a significant issue when it was found in later studies that some creatures had previously been given names and not in Hebrew. Andrew Dickson White noted that discoveries in Egypt showed the likenesses of various animals with their names in hieroglyphics and at a period long before the date of Creation established by the Christian church. Further studies revealed that, in the folklore of China, the sacred books concluded that animals were named by Fohi and in the Chinese language.

The beginning of the end of the language myth came in the seventeenth century, from a Professor Hottinger:

> The beginnings of a scientific theory seemed weak indeed, but they were none the less effective. As far back as 1661, Hottinger, professor at Heidelberg, came into the chorus of theologians like a great bell in a chime; but like a bell whose opening tone is harmonious and whose closing tone is discordant. For while, at the beginning, Hottinger cites a formidable list of great scholars who had held the sacred theory of the origin of language, he goes on to note a closer resemblance to the Hebrew in some languages than in others, and explains this by declaring that the confusion of tongues was of two sorts, total and partial: the Arabic and Chaldaic he thinks underwent only a partial confusion; the Egyptian, Persian, and all the European languages a total one. Here comes in the discord; here gently sounds forth from the great chorus a new note—that idea of grouping and classifying languages which at a later day was to destroy utterly the whole sacred theory.[2]

The discovery of Sanskrit brought to the world a new understanding of language. No longer could the multiplication of language be associated with the Tower of Babel, and now, even the divine origin of language came into doubt as evidence mounted that language resulted from a process of natural growth—evolution again.

Finally, it was Leibnitz (1646-1716) who declared, "There is as much reason for supposing Hebrew to have been the primitive language of mankind as there is for adopting the view of Goropius, who published a work at Antwerp in 1580 to prove that Dutch was the language spoken in paradise."[3]

Language was one aspect of culture that the ancients attributed to their gods, but the gods were finally portrayed as identical in most respects to those who worshipped them. The gods spoke the same language, shared the same features, lived in the area, dressed in the fashion, enjoyed local foods, and held the same prejudices against neighboring tribes and nations. In personality, as well, the gods were credited with traits that were found in ordinary men and women and thus were their quirks and caprices easier to understand. The gods, then, were made in the image of humans and, in particular, were consistent with the culture in question. Religious history reports no incidents where Hebrew gods spoke to their people in Arabic, nor where the gods of ancient Pacific Islanders were attired in double-breasted suits. The gods were products of the human imagination and, as such, possessed the characteristics of their inventors.

Of course, gods were not the only spirits cast in the mold of their constituencies—demons were as well. For example, only Christian demons could inhabit Christian bodies, and demons of other denominations were excluded. This permitted the Christian exorcist to deal with the situation, whereas he would have had no real control over non-Christian spirits of evil intent. Exorcism did require a measure of communication between the exorcist and the demon, which would have been difficult in a foreign language. The subsequent negotiation, as well, required that the demon verbally acknowledge the superior power of the Christian God and arrange to depart from the stricken person's body on a date that was agreeable to both parties in the negotiation. So both gods and demons necessarily took on the language and colorations of their cultures, and this was true of religions around the world, including the Christian religion.

Philology, then, finally demolished the Tower of Babel, one of the beliefs that have existed for thousands of years and only recently have come to be recognized as myths, not truths.

Notes

[1] Andrew Dickson White, *A History of the Warfare of Science with Theology in Christendom*, vol. 2 (New York: D. Appleton-Century, 1936), p. 169.

[2] Ibid., p. 189.

[3] Ibid., p. 190.

17

MYTHOLOGY: AND SO THE SERPENT SAID

The origin of language was one of the many religious myths that Christians and Jews adapted from earlier religions. Myths, of course, served as imaginative answers to questions when no knowledgeable answers were available. Scholars have now made it possible to trace the origin of many religious myths, which have guided our beliefs for centuries. For example the following:

- The story of Moses and the bulrushes belonged to a common stock of ancient tradition. The same story was told of the Accadian king Sargon who lived a thousand years before Moses.

- The story of Noah and the ark was found to be taken from an earlier Chaldean legend, in complete detail, including boarding the animals two by two.

- The Garden of Eden, the mystical tree, and the talking serpent were all known in pre-Semitic days, long before they appeared in the Bible as our explanation of evil.

- The six days of creation and the seventh day of rest shown in the scripture were of Babylonian origin—the very word *Sabbath* was of Babylonian origin.

¡qué poco originales!

- Scholars have found that the legends of the plagues of Egypt are mainly only exaggerations of natural occurrences that took place there every year, not miracles.

- The Ten Commandments have been found, in their ethical substance, in the earlier Egyptian *Book of the Dead* and so were not handed down by the Almighty.

- It now appears from early Egyptian texts that Egyptian myths were the source for Christian beliefs concerning trinities, miraculous conceptions, ascensions, resurrections, and more.

- Stories of the temptation of Christ by the devil have their counterparts in a number of religions whose deities were likewise tempted—including the "Temptation of Zoroaster."

- The ancient Persian religion, Zoroastrianism, also contributed legends concerning virgin births, miraculous conceptions, and the resurrection of the body, now found in Christian legends.

- Zoroastrianism originated the concept of Satan, who later became an essential part of Christian religious beliefs.

- Buddhism believes in the miraculous conception of Buddha and his virgin birth—true also of the god Horus in Egypt and Krishna in India, all of which preceded Christianity.

Because, in fact, so many of the miraculous happenings in the ancient world appeared to be shared by different religions in different countries, it finally became apparent that the stories were myths, not miracles. And comparative mythology, as a new science, had a vast collection of marvelous stories to consider. One example was the idea that various religious personages had left their imprint, usually on stones, before disappearing into the pages of history. Buddha's feet were said to be imprinted on stones in Siam and Ceylon; the body of

Moses imprinted near Mount Sinai; Poseidon's trident on the Acropolis at Athens; the hands of Christ on stones in France, Italy, and Palestine; the feet of Abraham on stones in Jerusalem and of Mohammed on a stone in a Cairo mosque; the devil's thighs on a rock in Brittany and his claws on stones in Germany; an imprint of the shoulder of the devil's grandmother at Mohrinersee; the little finger of Christ and the head of Satan at Ehrenberg; and the girdle of the Virgin Mother in Jerusalem.

There were many instances around the world when people were changed into stones, usually thought to betoken the anger of a god. And White notes that "while changes into stone or rock were considered punishments, or evidence of divine wrath, those into trees and shrubs were frequently looked upon as rewards, or evidences of divine favor."[1] These changes were seen in myths wherein Philemon became an oak tree; Baucis, a linden; Myrrha became myrtle; Melos, an apple tree; Attis, a pine tree; Adonis, a rose bush; the blood of the Titans became the vine and grape; and the blood of Hyacinthus, the hyacinth. Again, it was the commonality of such beliefs in various cultures and times that tended to type them as myths, not to mention the fact that society has outgrown such childish concepts.

As to Christian religious myths, Sir James Frazer, in his great work *Folklore in the Old Testament*, demonstrated beyond question that similar mythic tales are to be found in every quarter of this earth. A good example is the fact that Aztec, Mexico, even before the Catholic Spaniards arrived, worshipped a high god who was both remote and unbelievably powerful, together with "an incarnate Saviour, associated with a serpent, born of a virgin, who had died and was resurrected, one of whose symbols was a cross."[2] And Joseph Campbell noted that such legends of virgins giving birth to godlike persons who die and are then resurrected are commonplace around the world; long before Christianity, resurrection myths were present in the gods of Egypt, Mesopotamia, Syria, and Greece. So civilization has been prone to explain many of its mysteries by myths and has not failed to attribute marvelous qualities to its mythic heroes.

The death and resurrection of Attis, certainly, has a special significance to Christianity. He appeared to be a god of vegetation. His birth was said to be miraculous and his mother, Nana, a virgin. Frazer notes that tales about virgin births were "relics of an age of childlike ignorance when men had not yet recognized the intercourse of the sexes as the true cause of offspring."[3]

When Attis died each year, a period of mourning took place, but this was followed by a joyous celebration: "The sorrow of the worshipers was turned to joy. For suddenly a light shone in the darkness: the tomb was opened; the god has risen from the dead; and as the priest touched the lips of the weeping mourners with balm, he softly whispered in their ears the glad tidings of salvation. The resurrection of the god was hailed by his disciples as a promise that they too would issue triumphant from the corruption of the grave. On the morrow, the twenty-fifth day of March, which was reckoned the vernal equinox, the divine resurrection was celebrated with a wild outburst of glee."[4] As it happened, the resurrection of Christ paralleled rather closely the resurrection of Attis, which gave pause to the worshippers of that time:

> In point of fact it appears from the testimony of an anonymous Christian, who wrote in the fourth century of our era, that Christians and pagans alike were struck by the remarkable coincidence between the death and resurrection of their respective deities, and that the coincidence formed a theme of bitter controversy between the adherents of the rival religions, the pagans contending that the resurrection of Christ was a spurious imitation of the resurrection of Attis, and the Christians asserting with equal warmth that the resurrection

of Attis was a diabolical counterfeit of the resurrectio
Christ. In these unseemly bickerings the heathen took wh:
a superficial observer might seem strong ground by arguing
that their god was the older and therefore presumably the
original, not the counterfeit, since as a general rule an original
is older than its copy. This feeble argument the Christians easily
rebutted. They admitted, indeed, that in point of time Christ
was the junior deity, but they triumphantly demonstrated his
real seniority by falling back on the subtlety of Satan, who on
so important an occasion had surpassed himself by inverting
the usual order of nature.[5]

Today, one may marvel that people in all walks of life would
believe in the dead returning to life or in a literal Garden of Eden, a
serpent that could talk, and a fruit with marvelous properties—and for
thousands of years. But such is the nature of myths and legends and,
as Joseph Campbell says, "Today we know—and know right well—that
there was never anything of the kind: no garden of Eden anywhere on
this earth, no time when the serpent could talk, no prehistoric 'Fall,'
no exclusion from the garden, no universal flood, no Noah's Ark. The
entire history on which our leading occidental religions have been
founded is an anthology of fictions. But these are fictions of a type
that have had—curiously enough—a universal vogue as the founding
legends of other religions, too. Their counterparts have turned up
everywhere—and yet, there was never such a garden, serpent, tree or
deluge."[6]

When Joseph Campbell notes the nature of these beliefs, he asks the
questions that necessarily come to mind: "How do we account for such
anomalies? Who invents these impossible tales? Where do their images
come from? And why—though obviously absurd—are they everywhere
so reverently believed?" Only in the last several centuries, perhaps,

Jonah and the Whale

Joseph Campbell noted that the story of "Jonah and the Whale" was one example of a recurring mythic theme, almost universal, where the hero enters a fish's belly and comes out transformed.

(Culver Pictures, Inc.)

Religious myths are pure fantasy.

has our learning given us insight into the nature of our myths. A likely explanation is that because of the basic similarity of the human mind, people everywhere, when faced with questions concerning the origin of the world and everything in it, are likely to develop broadly similar answers. Such answers serve to articulate and integrate members into their culture and into a harmony of interrelatedness with the world in which they live.

Creation myths are characterized by the belief that all things natural were created by supernatural beings. The elaboration of such Creation myths in different societies constitutes an essential part of every religion together with its associated rituals. Reinforced by time and fortified by tradition, such myths become powerful institutions of social control and the structuring of reality. As such, religion constitutes perhaps the best example of the social construction of reality.

Myths, then, are themes of the imagination that address the most basic concerns of our existence. They speak to our concerns about mortality and suggest a different way to look at death, even to the point of suggesting the possibility of an eternal life. Myths also help the individual relate to a particular cultural setting by establishing a common denominator of belief, which then enfolds the individual. And finally, myths serve to answer all the unanswerable questions about the universe—those which bear on our ability to survive in an unknown environment.

So religious myths—themes of the imagination—are not to be despised even when they are pure fantasy. They serve, in effect, as placeholders until a scientific truth comes along. They merely represent an imaginative answer to a question that cannot, at a point in time, be answered in a more factual and satisfying manner. Particularly in the ancient world, the religious myth was the only means available to deal with questions on human origins, propensities, and the circumstance of death.

Adam and Eve

Christianity shared with many traditions the need to reconcile an all-powerful creator with an imperfect world, as in the magic garden.

(Detroit Free Press)

An example is the attempt by ancient peoples to reconcile an all-powerful creator with his end product—an imperfect world. Similarly, in the Christian tradition, we have attempted to reconcile the presence of God with the existence of evil, by means of a magic garden, a talking serpent, and an overcurious couple. Science has saved us from this conception, but the story of Adam and Eve served as an explanation of evil when no other was to be had.

So religion had answered many of life's questions with fanciful explanations, myths, most of which had been taken from more ancient religious cults when they too had been asked to explain the nature of the universe. The answers, then, first came from people who lived thousands of years ago in caves and huts and who were unable to explain natural phenomena other than to suppose that unseen spirits were at work. It was a theory of the universe that held invisible beings responsible for all the workings of the world. And the myths surrounding these figures have lasted for thousands of years.

Notes

[1] Andrew Dickson White, *A History of the Warfare of Science with Theology in Christendom*, vol. 2 (New York: D. Appleton-Century, 1936), p. 219.

[2] Joseph Campbell, *Myths to Live By* (New York: Bantam Books, 1973), p. 7.

[3] Sir James G. Frazer, *The Golden Bough*, vol. 1, abridged ed. (New York: Macmillan Publishing, 1922), p. 403.

[4] Ibid., p. 407.

[5] Ibid., p. 419.

[6] Campbell, *Myths to Live By*, p. 24.

[7] Stephen Jay Gould, *The Mismeasure of Man* (New York: W. W. Norton, 1981), p. 330.

18

PSYCHOLOGY: THE FUTURE OF AN ILLUSION

Sigmund Freud (1856-1939) has described religion as an illusion and noted that the "characteristic of illusions is that they are derived from human wishes."[1] In the simplest of terms, therefore, Freud held religion to be wishful thinking on the part of a beleaguered humanity.

From the beginning, humanity was virtually helpless against the onslaughts of nature, which came in the form of famine, flood, drought, quake, storm, plague, aging, and death. To early peoples and ancient civilizations, these natural phenomena were fearful events, beyond either explanation or control. Today, at least, humans understand some of the forces at work, even if their control is still limited.

In their attempts to explain natural phenomena, the imagination of primitive tribes did not go far beyond their own known abilities. So natural phenomena were explained as the work of activating spirits—beings such as themselves, but infinitely more powerful and, of course, invisible. Thus rain was water sprinkled by a heavenly spirit in much the same way as human beings sprinkled water. And lest this belief of early peoples seem naive, it may be remembered that, thousands of years later, the fathers of the Christian church still thought that rain came from a huge cistern in the sky and was released by angels who opened and closed the windows of heaven.

The invention of gods and spirits, then, was in large part a result of early human's need to understand and control the environment. And they proceeded to give their gods identities and personalities that would make them easier to understand and manage. Freud described the process: "The humanization of nature is derived from the need to put an end to man's perplexity and helplessness in the face of its dreaded forces, to get into a relation with them and finally to influence them."[2] Freud also suggested that the humanization process reflected an infantile model, wherein people had learned as children how to relate to and influence the persons with whom they came in contact.

So the gods were usually made in the image of humans—often from the standpoint of appearance and always from the standpoint of personality. The gods were powerful, but when given human personalities, they became familiar, controllable, and even vulnerable. They could be tempted, appeased, bribed, and sometimes threatened by their human constituents. Freud called it a replacement "of natural science by psychology,"[3] or wishful thinking, which provided immediate psychic relief from the threat of natural phenomena where no scientific defense was at hand.

If the humanization of the gods was a useful step in dealing with them, there was a role model that gave the gods an even more specific persona—they became father figures. Freud observed that the mother is the first to satisfy the child's need for love and often the "first protection against anxiety." But with respect to protection, Freud notes, "In this function [of protection] the mother is soon replaced by the stronger father, who retains that position for the rest of childhood. But the child's attitude to its father is coloured by a peculiar ambivalence. The father himself constitutes a danger for the child, perhaps because of its earlier relation to its mother. Thus it fears him no less than it longs for him and admires him. The indications of this ambivalence in the attitude to the father are deeply imprinted in every religion, as was shown in *Totem and Taboo*. When the growing individual finds that he is destined to remain a child forever, that he can never do without protection against strange superior powers, he lends those powers the features belonging to the figure of his father; he creates for himself the gods whom he dreads, whom he seeks to propitiate, and whom he nevertheless entrusts with his own protection. Thus his longing for a father is a motive identical with his need for protection against the consequences of his human weakness. The defence against childish helplessness is what lends its characteristic features to the adult's reaction to the helplessness which he has to acknowledge—a reaction which is precisely the formation of religion."[4]

Freud believed, then, that god-representations are based on the character of the father and reflect the dependency and helplessness not only of the child, but of the adult who soon comes to realize his or her vulnerability and, certainly, mortality.

Ana-Maria Rizzuto, in her *The Birth of the Living God*,[5] noted the resemblance of religious beliefs to such traditional objects as a child's teddy bear or blanket, which provide the child with a link between the familiar and the strange, the self, and the external world at a time when the child is trying to adapt to its environment. The god-representation in religion may provide a similar sense of security and well-being that can be sustained through a lifetime.

Religious beliefs are also sustained by other psychic rewards, such as reconciling one to his or her lot in life, together with assurances that any injustices will be corrected and any hardships compensated for, in this life or the next. It is a striking fact, observes Freud, that all religious ideas are exactly what we would wish them to be. And so their origin may be summed up:

> The psychical origin of religious ideas. These, which are given out as teachings, are not precipitates of experience or end results of thinking: they are illusions, fulfilments of the oldest, strongest and most urgent wishes of mankind. The secret of their strength lies in the strength of those wishes. As we already know, the terrifying impression of helplessness in childhood aroused the need for protection—for protection through love—which was provided by the father; and the recognition that this helplessness lasts throughout life made it necessary to cling to the existence of a father, but this time a more powerful one. Thus the benevolent rule of a divine Providence allays our fear of the dangers of life; the establishment of a moral world-order ensures the fulfilment of the demands of justice, which have so often remained unfulfilled in human civilization; and the prolongation of earthly existence in a future life provides the local and temporal framework in which these wishfulfilments shall take place.[6]

This perception of the origin of religious ideas is clearly different from the theological suggestion of a divine origin, wherein the gods of history spoke to and through their prophets who, in turn, revealed the identity of the god, his divine nature, and set forth his guidelines for an earthly existence and eternal reward.

A number of psychologists would disagree with Freud on some of his theories concerning religion, and Freud himself acknowledges that theories can and should change; Freud described his own theories as "scaffolding," on which to build, certainly not as eternal truths. But whatever the current disagreements, there is a consensus among psychologists on the substance of Freud's thoughts, namely, that religion is a mental product that is not beholden to supernatural beings.

Freud devoted his book *The Future of an Illusion* to the idea that religion and a belief in spirits was wishful thinking and an illusion that would eventually be displaced. He concluded his book with this counterpoint: "No, our science is not illusion. But an illusion it would be to suppose that what science cannot give us we can get elsewhere."[7]

The disposition to indulge in wishful thinking is certainly characteristic of humans around the world and has been evident through the ages. Even the youngest children have shown the tendency to indulge in fantasies of wish fulfillment. St. Nicholas is the recognized name in this respect, wherein Santa Claus gives children the hope that all their wishes will be answered by a powerful benefactor. In some ways, the child's belief in Santa Claus is a youthful version of a later belief in God. The parallel begins with the idea that Santa will grant whatever requests are made of him, and if the red bicycle is not there on Christmas morning, the oversight is soon forgotten and the request made again the following year. Santa is able to overcome all limitations of time and space and cover the entire world in a single evening—in effect, be everywhere at once. And although billions of children must be heard, Santa is able to give each child the individual attention that he or she requires. But there is also a sterner side to Santa, and the child had better be good or may stand to lose his or her hoped-for rewards. All in all, then, children are offered a fantasy that enables them to seek their heart's desire.

Of course, the scientific community does not believe in St. Nicholas because such a figure runs counter to personal experience and reason. Santa has never been experienced; his reported exploits have never been proved and certainly do not stand the test of reason. And besides,

Sigmund Freud

Sigmund Freud held that a belief in a spirit world was an illusion born of wishful thinking. Today, most psychologists would agree.

Con el permiso de Freud: ¡ Que vaste tu chiquita! por favor; ¿¡ no sabes que hay muchas dimensiones en este y otros universos ? el "spirit world" es una de esas muchas.

children have always been apt to indulge in fantasies of wish fulfillment. For these same reasons, most scientists do not believe in a spirit world. In the case of psychologists, a 1972 survey of members of the American Psychological Association showed that fewer than 2 percent were theists.

Notes

1   Sigmund Freud, *The Future of an Illusion* (New York: W. W. Norton, 1961), p. 31.

2   Ibid., p. 22.

3   Ibid., p. 17.

4   Ibid., p. 24.

5   Ana-Maria Rizzuto, *The Birth of the Living God* (Chicago: University of Chicago Press, 1979).

6   Freud, *The Future of an Illusion*, p. 30.

7   Ibid., p. 56.

19

SUMMARY

Understanding the Universe

To early humans, the natural world was both a shadow and a splendor. Nature was a resource that provided food, shelter, and other elements of survival, but then nature unleashed the terrible forces of flood, famine, drought, windstorm, and quake. It followed that humans sought an understanding of the laws and vagaries of the natural world.

Some scholars have noted three systems of thought that have attempted to explain the natural world. Animism was the earliest attempt. Unable to explain natural phenomena in any other way, early peoples assumed the presence of activating spirits. In humans, for example, the difference between a live body and a dead body was thought to be a spirit that powered the body; the spirit within was usually smaller, necessarily insubstantial to allow movement through the body and, although invisible, very human in its supposed appearance.

In time, animals and other life-forms and, finally, inanimate objects were all thought to be possessed by spirits. As Comte stated in his law of wills and causes, "When men do not know the natural causes of things, they simply attribute them to wills like their own; thus they obtain a theory which provisionally takes the place of science."[1] And so all things in nature were invested with spirits, and humankind had a comprehensive, if mistaken, explanation for the workings of the world.

Animism was followed by religion, which gave structure and sophistication to the earlier belief in spirits and offered a ruling body of gods. But religion also carried forward a number of animistic beliefs for thousands of years. Even today, a Hindu believes that cows are sacred and the waters of the Ganges can purify souls. The Muslim reveres the Black Stone of Mecca, a fallen meteorite. A Shinto believes his emperor is a descendant of the sun-god Amaterasu. A Christian believes in angelic figures that are part animal and part human in form. So animism lives but now under the roof of religious beliefs, and religion has emerged as the second system of thought concerning the nature of the universe. Science has become the third.

Bertrand Russell defined science as "the attempt to discover, by means of observation, and reasoning based upon it, first, particular facts about the world, and then laws connecting facts with one another and (in fortunate cases) making it possible to predict future occurrences."[2] This approach distinguished science from animism and religion, both of which supposed that invisible beings had orchestrated the universe.

And it seems clear that science, in a few centuries, has given us knowledge that thousands of years of religious surmise has failed to produce. The reason is that science offered the evidence of its findings while the proofs of religion were scanty indeed, once causing Bertrand Russell to remark, "The kind of god that I believe in would disown most of the human race for believing in him on insufficient evidence."

three systems of thought that have attempted to explain the natural world:
1) Animism - all things in nature are invested with spirits
2) Religion
3) Science

On Science and Religion

Perhaps unexpectedly, then, science and religion have both had the same goal: to serve humanity through a better understanding of the universe. Were science and religion on different tracks, a confrontation might have been avoided. But each system of thought has traveled the same ground and explained the universe in its own, and very different, terms.

The difference between science and religion, then, is not a difference in objectives but of approach. Ashley Montagu summarized it well:

It is an interesting reflection that this craving to relate oneself to the mysterious forces of the universe, to reveal and to bring into harmonic order something of its mystery, is precisely the same attitude of mind to which we give the name "scientific." It is in the means, the method, by which these attitudes are realized that the difference between science and religion are produced. The method of religion is private acquiescence in the public solution of the mystery, whereas science is characterized by public acquiescence in the private solution of the mystery. Religion is a social communion in which the individual joins; science is essentially the continuous creation of the individuals who have privately pursued their devotions but who have had to submit to having them publicly verified before they could be accepted. The method of religion is faith; the method of science is doubt. Faith is certainty without proof. Science is proof without certainty. Religion as experience is subjective; science as experience is objective—or at least attempts to be. Religion is revelatory; science is demonstrative. But when all this has been said, even at these areas of difference the resemblances between religion and science are substantial.[3]

Today, the source of the conflict between science and religion centers on the ancient teachings of the Church and the fact that most men and women believe as did their ancestors, thousands of years ago, when people were prone to believe the most fanciful stories. Even at the time of Christ, the Roman generals believed in sacred chickens, whose pecking demeanor augured well or ill for a coming military engagement. Our own religious beliefs were passed down from civilizations much earlier than that; we can look to Babylon or before to find the roots of our religious beliefs, which were born in an age of superstition and have persisted to this day with little change in substance.

The enduring quality of our religious beliefs was probably a natural consequence of believing in a god who was omniscient, omnipotent, and omnibenevolent—for with such guidance one would suppose that there was little to do other than cultivate the good graces of this supreme being. And the early fathers of the Christian church certainly expressed the opinion, in the strongest possible terms, that the Bible contained all there was to know—at least that God wanted humans to know—about the nature of things.

And so religion attributed all natural phenomena to the work of the Almighty, thought to be a gigantic man clad in a flowing robe, whose throne was surrounded by hosts of winged angels. At night he hung out the stars and, at daybreak, set the sun on its journey across the sky, which was stretched like a skin overhead, supported by a ring of mountains that rose above a flat earth. Heaven was above the sky and hell in the fiery bowels of the earth. And the wishes of the Almighty were made known to mankind by comets flung across the night sky or by his booming voice in a thunderclap.

One may reflect that this was a childlike view of the universe. But it may be remembered that the entire panorama of religious belief began in cultures that were just emerging from the Stone Age. Thus there were stories in sacred scripture of the dead who returned to life, virgins who gave birth, water that was turned into wine, sticks that were turned into snakes, humans who talked with gods, and humans who were also gods. Most of these stories began ten thousand years ago, or more, when humankind had not yet risen above superstitious fancies and clung to some incredible explanations of the natural world, centering on a world of invisible beings. *¡ qué por... hemos sido !*

Over fifty years ago, Sigmund Freud concluded that belief in a spirit world was mere wishful thinking, and today, most scientists would share the conclusion as stated in his *Civilization and its Discontents*: "The whole thing is so patently infantile, so foreign to reality, that to anyone with a friendly attitude to humanity it is painful to think that the great majority of mortals will never be able to rise above this view of life."[4]

The Primacy of Science

The Church was well aware that its credibility was at stake in its explanation of the natural world, which had been described as the work of a powerful spirit. In effect, the Church asked, "How else can one explain the sun's movement across the heavens unless it is propelled by an invisible being—a spirit?" And so it was that the physical universe tended to confirm the presence of spirits. If the natural world was otherwise explained, however, there would be no basis for a belief in spirits or in a god. And science had begun to explain the universe in terms of natural, not supernatural causes.

Some would say that religion's concept of the universe began to crumble in 1492 with the voyage of Columbus, for his voyage—and those of Vasco da Gama and Magellan—gave convincing evidence that the earth was round and populated on the opposite side, and thus, religion was wrong, at least in one respect. As it happened, religion was to be proved wrong in many respects concerning the nature of the universe.

- Astronomy showed that the earth was not the center of the universe nor did God trundle out the stars each night.

- Geology produced evidence of fossil life which predated the religious assumption of Creation by a wide margin.

- Meteorology showed that weather was not the function of a divine will, used for punishments and rewards, and controllable by church bells.

- Biology showed that humans had not been created from nothing, in the wink of any eye, but evolved through the ages—and from other animals.

- Anthropologists compared human cultures and documented the upward progression of civilization—with no attendant record of a biblical Fall.

- Philology revealed that language had evolved around the world and was not attributable to a jealous God who scattered the builders of the Towel of Babel.

- Medical studies revealed that illnesses and emotional disturbances were not the work of demons who could be coaxed from their habitats by exorcists.

- Scholars discovered that ancient Egyptians were the source of many Jewish and Christian beliefs, such as the brazen serpent, golden calf, miraculous conceptions, ascensions, resurrections, incarnations, virgin births, diabolical influences, and more.

- Mythology confirmed the striking occurrence that most Christian beliefs were taken from more primitive civilizations whose beliefs, in turn, were grounded in superstitions.

- Psychology has shown that a disposition to believe in a spirit world may come from a sense of dependency we experience as children and never outgrow. Gods and goddesses appear to be themes of the imagination that have been modeled on our own fathers and mothers.

So many religious beliefs that began millennia ago have been toppled by the advance in learning, brought about through science. And perhaps the assurance—even pride—that was felt in following ancient traditions is now being questioned. Some argue that belief requires more direct and objective evidence or, as Weston La Barre puts it, "Inevitably, each man often must discriminate between what he has been taught and what he has learned. He must make his peace with the past, his own and that of the race, and choose at times between the wisdom of the fathers and his own direct experience. This is the method of daily common sense and of science."[5]

The Impact on Religion

The ascendancy of science in our century has brought with it a natural concern over the loss of traditional religious beliefs. For the better part of two thousand years, the Christian world has been guided by a set of beliefs that were thought to be of divine origin and therefore indisputable. Enter science, and in a few centuries, all the Church's notions about the physical world have been set aside and the very foundation of Christian belief—the existence of a spirit world—has been challenged. These developments have caused concern, rightly enough, and encouraged another look at the benefits and detriments of religious beliefs.

Certainly religion has been a mixed blessing over the years, and there is something to be said on either side of the equation. Simply put:

Human Goodness: Religion has provided the world with an ideal of human conduct, consistent with the cultural settings involved, and has encouraged its attainment. At the same time, religion has often set a disappointing moral example through its long-standing prejudices and harsh persecutions.

Human Endeavor: Religion has given inspiration to many people and values beyond life's material considerations. Yet religion has severely repressed intellectual endeavor, particularly where the knowledge challenged the authority of the church.

Human Anxiety: Religion has offered some freedom from worry based on a belief in the protection of supernatural beings. But religion has also created anxiety through a calculated fear of sex, sin, demons, and eternal damnation.

Human Adversity: Religion provides the hope (even the assurance) that suffering and privation may be overcome in this life and perhaps rewarded in the next. But such expectations may be illusory and encourage people to accept their present lot in life.

Human Bonding: There is a bond that joins members of the same faith—a community of beliefs that extends from cradle to grave with overtones of a shared eternity. And yet this bonding has often resulted in prejudice against nonbelievers and so stops short of a deep regard for all humanity.

On balance, Freud believed that people would be better off without religion, if only from the standpoint that reality is healthier than illusion in our lives. Even so, many are concerned that an interruption in our religious beliefs would result in chaos. The concern is that humanity has been taught that its basic behavioral guidelines come from gods so that if the gods go, their guidelines may go with them, with chaos the result.

The concern over chaos, however, may not take into account fully the change in religious beliefs that has already begun. The trickle of disbelief that began in the fifteenth and sixteenth centuries has become more of a tide in the twentieth century, and yet people seem to have adapted, perhaps by having more faith in themselves and in science. The adaptation is underway, in any case, and many of our ancient religious beliefs are no longer credited by the Christian laity and, in many cases, by the clergy. When the beliefs are taken as a group, a marked change in the Christian outlook is apparent:

- The bedrock of Christian morality, the Ten Commandments, are no longer thought to have been written by the hand of God, but taken from an early Egyptian document.

- The Bible stories that inspired our childhood are now widely recognized as religious myth: the Garden of Eden, the Tower of Babel, Noah and the ark, Jonah and the whale, and Moses in the bulrushes.

- The awesome creatures that once filled our Christian skies are now remnants of a bygone age: ghosts, witches, dragons, angels, imps, devils, and demons of varied description.

- The infallibility of the pope has been questioned, evident in that birth control (called vicious by Pope Pius XI) is now accepted by most Christian laity and many clergy.

- Such essential elements of the Christian faith, as the virgin birth and the resurrection of Jesus, have been disputed by a group of eminent Bible scholars, called the Jesus Seminar.

- The ancient belief that demons inhabit the body but can be exorcised has been called an "embarrassment" by a prominent Catholic theologian.

- The belief that bread and wine miraculously become the body and blood of Christ (transubstantiation) was rejected in earlier years by Protestants and is now thought by most Catholics to be symbolic rather than real.

- Some of the most revered Christian saints, such as St. Christopher and St. George, have recently been dropped from the rolls of the Catholic Church because of their doubtful historicity.

- The miracles attributed to thousands of Christian saints are now questioned by many lay and religious observers: levitation, bilocation, changing shape, raising the dead, and hanging cloaks on sunbeams.

Many of the aforementioned are the foundational beliefs of Christianity, such as the bodily resurrection of Jesus. If Jesus was not resurrected according to scriptural accounts, then the Bible is in error and the divinity of Christ is disputable—and our own hopes for a resurrection greatly diminished. And yet this is the conclusion of some of the country's most eminent Biblical scholars. It is significant, also, that the conclusion comes from the theological side rather than the scientific, suggesting a more open-minded attitude in all circles of our society.

One of the more significant changes in the Christian outlook was announced by Pope John Paul II in 1999 when he declared that hell was not a real place but rather a state of mind among those who had separated themselves from God. One may then ask whether the devil is not also a figure existing only in the imagination—and wonder whether, one day, heaven may similarly be declared a state of mind.

Most of the beliefs that have fallen from favor are those of a miraculous turn and those that are dependent on the appearance and antics of bizarre creatures. Such drama, perhaps, played better in earlier centuries among audiences attuned to the fantasia of the times. Today, the findings of science are replacing the fantasies of early religious beliefs, wherein feathered angels circled high above, evil demons lurked below, and miraculous events were a common occurrence. The dilemma is that religion as we know it cannot easily sever itself from the founding concept of Christianity, that invisible beings (of whatever description) exist in the world and may be dealt with by humans.

So science has challenged religious beliefs about the universe, the earth, humanity, and finally has given a view of religion as a product not of a spirit world but of the human mind. It may be appropriate, then, to note this conclusion of Sigmund Freud: "In the long run nothing can withstand reason and experience, and the contradiction which religion offers to both is all too palpable. Even purified religious ideas cannot escape this fate, so long as they try to preserve anything of the consolation of religion. No doubt if they confine themselves to a belief in a higher spiritual being, whose qualities are indefinable and whose purposes cannot be discerned, they will be proof against the challenge of science; but then they will also lose their hold on human interest."[6]

A Perspective on the Future

We have seen that religious ideas and the creation of gods are thought to be psychical in origin and are, in essence, wishful thinking on the part of humans. In this respect, science and religion have shared a common goal in that both attempt to satisfy human needs—religion through the creation of gods and science through the empowerment of humans. Seemingly, science has been the more successful in that humans have been empowered to the point that our current abilities would appear godlike to ancient peoples.

In his book *Civilization and its Discontents,* written in 1930, Freud noted that humans of that era had significantly improved, if not perfected, their motor and sensory organs. Powerful engines had increased their muscularity and placed giant forces at their disposal. Spectacles, telescopes, and microscopes had improved their vision and extended its limits. Telephones and other auditory devices had improved their hearing and extended its range across continents. Cameras and auditory recording devices had given them powers of recollection that went well beyond the human memory. These assets were cultural acquisitions, not related to religion, and yet gave to humans many powers that once were sought from their gods:

> All these assets he may lay claim to as his cultural acquisition. Long ago he formed an ideal conception of omnipotence and omniscience which he embodied in his gods. To these gods he attributed everything that seemed unattainable to his wishes, or that was forbidden to him. One may say, therefore, that these gods were cultural ideals. Today he has come very close to the attainment of his ideal, he has almost become a god himself. Only, it is true, in the fashion in which ideals are usually attained according to the general judgment of humanity. Not completely; in some respects not at all, in others only half way. Man has, as it were, become a kind of prosthetic God. When he puts on all his auxiliary organs he is truly magnificent; but those organs have not grown on to him and they still give him much trouble at times. Nevertheless, he is entitled to console himself with the thought that this development will not come to an end precisely with the year 1930 AD. Future ages will bring with them new and probably unimaginably great advances in this field of civilization and will increase man's likeness to God still more.[7]

No doubt our civilization's new use of computers to supplement human brain power, television to enhance human communications, and our recent travel in space would qualify as advances which make humans more godlike. Television, in effect, gives a spokesperson the ability to be everywhere in the world at the same time, an ability once associated only with gods (or those saints who were favored with the gift of ubiquity). Interplanetary travel was once the province of angels, whose feathered wings and flappings may now appear to be antiquated modes of flight.

So human wishes are now being satisfied by science, by human endeavor and a greater understanding of human needs, and as a result, the ancient gods are not being called on as before. Mental and physical illnesses, for example, were once the responsibility of the gods (the causes and cures) to the extent that the priesthood, Christian and others, forbade the practice of medicine as an unseemly interference with a divine prerogative. Today, both priest and layperson rely on medical science to treat their mental and physical problems, and few believe that diseases, which are beyond our current reach, such as AIDS, will be cured by an appeal to unseen spirits.

Humanity, therefore, which in earlier ages created gods as a way to fulfill its urgent desires, now seeks fulfillment from science—a very human resource. Human wishes have shown themselves to be a powerful force then, strong enough to create a system of gods, which has never appealed to reason, and strong enough, also, to create a more viable alternative called science, which is now displacing the gods. So the origin of gods, and now their twilight, have both been brought about by the power of human wishes. And the transition from religion to science is now underway.

A closing thought on the subject is this: The good scientist will be alive to the fact that science is sometimes in danger of become a secular religion, whose brave new world may put an end to our species even more efficiently than the mythology of the true believer.

Notes

1   Andrew Dickson White, *A History of the Warfare of Science with Theology in Christendom,* vol. 2 (New York: D. Appleton-Century, 1936), p. 169.

2   Bertrand Russell, *Religion and Science* (New York: Oxford University Press, 1961), p. 8.

3   Ashley Montagu, *Immortality, Religion, and Morals* (New York: Hawthorn Books, 1971), p. 72.

4   Sigmund Freud, *Civilization and Its Discontents* (New York W. W. Norton, 1961), p. 21.

5   Weston La Barre, *The Ghost Dance* (New York: Doubleday, 1970), p. 3.

6   Sigmund Freud, *The Future of an Illusion* (New York: W. W. Norton, 1961), p. 54.

7   Freud, *Civilization and Its Discontents*, p. 38.

REFERENCES

Asimov, Isaac. *Beginnings*. New York: Berkley Books, 1989.

Berger, Peter L., and Thomas Luckmann. *The Social Construction of Reality*. Garden City, New York: Doubleday, 1966.

Campbell, Joseph. *Myths to Live By*. New York: Bantam Books, 1973.

Cavendish, Richard. *Man, Myth and Magic*. New York: Marshall Cavendish Corporation, 1983.

Cravens, Hamilton. *The Triumph of Evolution*. Philadelphia: University of Pennsylvania Press, 1978.

Darwin, Charles. *Origin of Species*. New York: Collier, 1901.

Dobzhansky, Theodosius, and Ashley Montagu. *Natural Selection and the Mental Capacities of Mankind. Science,* vol. 105, 1947.

Draper, John William. *History of the Conflict between Religion and Science*. New York: D. Appleton, 1902.

Frazer, James G. *Folklore in the Old Testament*. Abridged Edition. New York: Avenel Books, 1988.

Frazer, James G. *The Golden Bough*. Vol. 1. Abridged Edition. New York: Macmillan Publishing, 1922.

Freud, Sigmund. *Civilization and Its Discontents.*
New York: W. W. Norton, 1961.

Freud, Sigmund. *The Future of an Illusion.*
New York: W. W. Norton, 1961.

Freud, Sigmund. *Totem and Taboo.* New York: Vintage Books, 1946.

Funk, Robert W., and Roy W. Hoover. *The Five Gospels: The Search for the Authentic Words of Jesus.* New York: Macmillan Publishing, 1993.

Gould, Stephen Jay. *The Mismeasure of Man.*
New York: W. W. Norton, 1981.

Hastings, James. Editor *The Encyclopaedia Of Religion And Ethics.*
New York: Charles Scribner & Sons, 1951.

Hawking, Stephen W. *A Brief History of Time.*
New York: Bantam Books, 1988.

La Barre, Weston. *The Ghost Dance.* New York:
Doubleday & Company, 1970.

Leakey, Richard E. and Roger Lewin. *Origins.* New York: Dutton, 1977.

Montagu, Ashley. *Immortality, Religion and Morals.* New York: Hawthorn Books, 1971.

Montagu, Ashley. *Man's Most Dangerous Myth: The Fallacy of Race*—5th Edition. New York: Oxford University Press, 1974.

New Catholic Encyclopedia. New York: McGraw-Hill, 1967.

Rizzuto, Ana-Maria. *The Birth of The Living God.* Chicago: University of Chicago Press, 1979.

Russell, Bertrand. *Religion and Science.* New York: Oxford University Press, 1961.

U.S. News & World Report. "Who Wrote the Bible?" December 10, 1990.

White, Andrew Dickson *A History of the Warfare of Science with Theology In Christendom.* 2 vols. New York: D. Appleton-Century Company, 1936.

ILLUSTRATIONS

These sources have generously given permission for the use of these illustrations:

- Threefold God: By permission of the Master and Fellows of St. John's College, Cambridge, England.
- A Doomed World: Camera Press, Ltd., London.
- A Demon King: British Museum/Michael Holford, London.
- Witches on High: Dover Publications.
- A Rainbow's Promise: Dembinsky Photo Associates, Owosso, Michigan.
- The World Turns: From *The Way Things Work* by David Macaulay. Compilation copyright © 1988 by Dorling Kindersley, Ltd. Text copyright © 1988 by David Macaulay and Neil Ardley. Illustrations copyright © 1988 by David Macaulay. Reprinted by permission of Houghton Mifflin Co. All rights reserved.
- Nicolaus Copernicus: North Wind Pictures Archives, Alfred, Maine.
- Galileo Galilei: Art Resource, New York City, New York.
- The Hand of God: From *The Way Things Work* by David Macaulay. Compilation copyright © 1988 by Dorling Kindersley, Ltd. Text copyright © 1988 by David Macaulay and Neil Ardley. Illustrations

- Instruments of Torture: Mansell Collection/Time Pix; used in Bamberg witch trials, seventeenth century.

- Witch-Finder General: Mary Evans Picture Library, London.

- Ferdinand Magellan: The Granger Collection, New York.

- This Old World: Adapted from *Beginnings* by Isaac Asimov.

- Giants among Men: Reprinted with the permission of Simon and Schuster Children's Publishing Division from *The Macmillan Book of Greek Gods and Heros* by Alice Low, illustrated by Arvis Stewart. Copyright © 1985 Macmillan Publishing Company.

- Fall of Man: Folk Art Museum, Michigan State University. Nature Studies: Smithsonian Institution Libraries, © 2001 Smithsonian Institution.

- An Ape Man: © Ardea, London; *The Hornet,* March 1871.

- The Alchemist: Mansell Collection/Time Pix.

- Ben Franklin: North Wind Picture Archives, Alfred, Maine.

- Body by Vesalius: The Library of Royal College of Surgeons of England, England.

- The Deluge: Erich Lessing/Art Resource, New York City, New York.

- The Tower of Babel: The British Library, Special Collections, London; from the *Bedford Book of Hours*, fifteenth century.

- Jonah and the Whale: Culver Pictures, New York City, New York.

- Adam and Eve: Taken from *Detroit Free Press*, August 22, 1990.

- Sigmund Freud: The Library of Congress, Washington, DC.

- Adam and Eve (cover): The British Library, London, UK.

- Prophet Ezekiel: Cincinnati Art Museum.

- Ascending Soul: Mary Evans Picture Library, London.

- Saint Brendan: Mary Evans Picture Library, London.

- Healing Gods: Hulton Getty Picture Collection, England.

- Early Communion: Mary Evans Picture Library, London.

- Early Goddess: August C. Long Health Science Library, Columbia University, New York City, New York.

- Ancient Supplicants: The Oriental Institute of the University of Chicago.

- Christ's Resurrection: Courtesy of Museo Civico, Sansepolero, Italy.

- Anthony's Demons: The British Museum, London.

Quotations

The publishers have generously given permission to use extended quotations from the following copyrighted works:

From *Folklore in the Old Testament* by Sir James George Frazer, by permission of A. P. Watt Ltd. on behalf of The Council of Trinity College, Cambridge.

From *The Future of Illusion* by Sigmund Freud, translated by James Strachey. Copyright © 1961 by James Strachey, renewed 1989 by Alex Strachey. Used by permission W. W. Norton & Co., Inc.

From *Who Wrote the Bible?* Copyright © December 10, 1990, *US News and World Report.* Reprinted by permission of the publisher.

From *The Five Gospels* review, reprinted by permission of *The St. Petersburg Times.*

"It Ain't Necessarily So," Music and lyrics by George Gershwin, DuBois and Dorothy Heyward, and Ira Gershwin. Copyright © 1935 (Renewed 1962) George Gershwin Music, Ira Gershwin Music, and DuBose and Dorothy Heyward Memorial Fund. All rights administered by WB Music Corp. All rights reserved. Used by permission, Warner Bros. Publication US Inc., FL 33014.